"If I am terrible at this, I will happily go sit by the pool."

"Are you asking me to give up on you before we even begin?" Brady asked.

Her lips twitched upward. "I would rather be told I can't go on the tour than ruin everyone else's time."

"You would have to have no ability to balance for me to give up on you."

"Okay, I think I have *some* balance." Immediately after those words left her mouth, she stumbled on an invisible trip hazard in the grass.

Brady reached for her arm to steady her. She grimaced then laughed. Her ability to laugh at herself was endearing. She had an infectious kind of giggle. Brady let go of her and had to shake off the weird tingles she was giving him. She was a guest at the inn, not someone for him to flirt with. "I believe in you, Ms. Fox."

"Alexa. You can call me Alexa."

"You got it, Alexa." He liked the way her name sounded. He shook his head and gave his neck a rub. *Guest, guest, guest*, he reminded himself.

Dear Reader,

I am so excited for the beginning of this new series for Harlequin Heartwarming. The Seasons Inn was a place I had dreamed up years ago, but it wasn't until the summer of 2023 when my husband and I traveled all around the New England states that I figured out exactly where this inn belonged.

Just like my vacation, the first story in the series is set in the summer. In *Her Summer to Start Over*, Brady and Alexa have very little in common when they first meet, but sometimes we need someone with different strengths to help us through the things we think we can't overcome. It also helps to have a meddling moose. What does that mean? You'll have to keep reading to find out!

Thank you for coming on this new journey with me. I can't wait for you to meet all the Seasons siblings. They each will have their own season to fall in love, and I hope you enjoy reading them all.

XOXO,

Amy Vastine

HER SUMMER TO START OVER

AMY VASTINE

Harlequin
HEARTWARMING

If you purchased this book without a cover you should be aware that this book is stolen property. It was reported as "unsold and destroyed" to the publisher, and neither the author nor the publisher has received any payment for this "stripped book."

Harlequin®
HEARTWARMING™

ISBN-13: 978-1-335-05157-8

Her Summer to Start Over

Copyright © 2025 by Amy Vastine

All rights reserved. No part of this book may be used or reproduced in any manner whatsoever without written permission.

Without limiting the author's and publisher's exclusive rights, any unauthorized use of this publication to train generative artificial intelligence (AI) technologies is expressly prohibited.

This is a work of fiction. Names, characters, places and incidents are either the product of the author's imagination or are used fictitiously. Any resemblance to actual persons, living or dead, businesses, companies, events or locales is entirely coincidental.

For questions and comments about the quality of this book, please contact us at CustomerService@Harlequin.com.

TM and ® are trademarks of Harlequin Enterprises ULC.

Harlequin Enterprises ULC
22 Adelaide St. West, 41st Floor
Toronto, Ontario M5H 4E3, Canada
www.Harlequin.com

Recycling programs for this product may not exist in your area.

Printed in U.S.A

Amy Vastine has been plotting stories in her head for as long as she can remember. An eternal optimist, she studied social work, hoping to teach others how to find their silver lining. Now she enjoys creating happily-ever-afters for all to read. Amy lives outside Chicago with her high school–sweetheart husband, three teenagers who keep her on her toes and their two sweet but mischievous pups. Visit her at amyvastine.com.

Books by Amy Vastine

Harlequin Heartwarming

The Blackwell Belles

A Cowgirl's Thanksgiving Kiss

Stop the Wedding!

A Marriage of Inconvenience
The Sheriff's Valentine
The Christmas Wedding Crashers
His Texas Runaway Bride

Return of the Blackwell Brothers

The Rancher's Fake Fiancée

The Blackwell Sisters

Montana Wishes

The Blackwells of Eagle Springs

A Wyoming Secret Proposal

Visit the Author Profile page
at Harlequin.com for more titles.

To my friend Jennifer.
I promised a book about what happens after.
Here's to finding your joy. You deserve it.

CHAPTER ONE

"I KNOW YOU'RE on vacation—"

"It's fine. Give me one minute to forward you those emails." Alexa Fox was determined to prove to the world that she could take an actual vacation and remember how to have fun...and she intended to do just that right after she finished sending these emails to her assistant, Neil.

It was a Friday afternoon and she was five and a half hours into a six-hour drive from Manhattan to New Hampshire. She'd attended three meetings virtually, made at least six phone calls during the drive, and dictated several emails while behind the wheel. This was the last thing she needed to do before she actually started her vacation.

"Roger will appreciate that you went above and beyond once again," Neil said, referring to Alexa's boss.

Roger Gatton was a billionaire who invested in companies based on the research Alexa and her colleagues did. Some might call him a corporate raider, but Alexa liked to think of him as a savvy businessman who, with her help, found ways to make other companies more profitable.

Was it bad that Gatton Investments usually profited the most or that many times the original owners had to watch the company they built be broken into parts and sold to the highest bidder? Okay, that part didn't always make her feel great about what she did for a living, but she had convinced herself that this was the world they lived in. True entrepreneurs understood that it wasn't personal, it was always business.

Alexa held her phone in one hand and gripped the steering wheel with the other. She was aware that being on her phone while driving was a bad idea, but it was just going to take a second. Plus, she was in the middle of nowhere and hadn't seen another car for miles.

"I'm also going to text Jordan about the Steel Masters presentation," Alexa said, taking her eyes off the road to open up her text messages. Jordan would be at work for a few more hours, just like she would have been had she not taken this vacation.

When she shifted her gaze back to the road, there was a humongous moose standing in the middle of it.

Alexa threw aside her phone and yanked the steering wheel to the right to avoid colliding with the animal. The tires screeched in unison with her as she slammed on the brakes. There was, however, no avoiding the inevitable as her rental car crashed into a tree. The airbag deployed and the seat belt locked, saving her life but punishing her body at the same time.

Alexa's heart pounded in her chest and adrenaline was surely coursing through her veins. Rattled, she took a moment to be sure she was all right. She was still in one piece and relatively unharmed. She opened the door and got out to assess the damage to the car. The front end was crumpled. Smoke rose from the dented hood.

The moose in the road made a noise as if it was trying to get her attention. She spun around to see it looking at her over its shoulder. It grunted and slowly made its way across the highway to the other side.

"I hope that was your way of saying sorry!" she shouted as it disappeared into the trees. This was just great. What kind of way was this to start a vacation that was supposed to be relaxing and carefree? Maybe it was the universe's way of telling her that her inability to disconnect from work wasn't only going to be the reason her marriage ended, but could also be the death of her if she wasn't careful.

She stood there for a moment, mentally going over the new list of problems to solve. How was she going to get to the inn? Walk? Were there rideshare drivers out here in the middle of nowhere? Where was her phone? She needed to call her insurance agent. She needed to call the car-rental company. Where was she going to find a tow truck?

Her missing phone rang from inside the car. Alexa pushed her blond hair from her face before she tried to yank open the passenger-side door. Neil was probably wondering why they'd gotten cut off. She got down on her knees to dig under the seat, where it sounded like the ring was coming from. Brett's face stared back at her when she retrieved it. Could this get any worse? Her ex-husband was calling? She slid her finger across the screen to answer it and braced herself for the conversation to come.

"Hey, Brett."

"Alexa? Are you messing with me?" He sounded annoyed.

"Why would I be messing with you? You called me."

"I just got an emergency text message from Crash Detection saying your phone had to call 911 from somewhere in New Hampshire and I'm being contacted because I'm listed as an emergency contact."

Shoot. Alexa had forgotten to remove him as her emergency contact. Embarrassment heated her cheeks. "Sorry about that. Darn phones have a mind of their own these days. I didn't know it could make calls and send texts by itself."

"Alexa," he said on a sigh. "You don't have to play these games."

Her embarrassment was quickly replaced by confusion. "Games?"

"We're divorced. I know it's hard not being in each other's lives anymore, but it's important to not create fake drama to get my attention."

Confusion shifted into anger. "Fake drama? I was in a car accident and my phone called you on its own. I'll remove you as my emergency contact as soon as we hang up. In fact..." She hung up and deleted his contact information all together.

Her skin prickled as it warmed. Brett had gotten a message that she had possibly been in an accident and instead of asking her if she was okay, he'd acted like she had done it to get his attention. How dare he accuse her of playing games. Her heartbeat sped up again, so she took a deep breath in an attempt to calm down.

Alexa and Brett had been married for ten years. They had been college sweethearts for two years before that. About nine months ago, he'd looked her in the face and told her that he felt nothing for her anymore and wanted a divorce. It still boggled her mind and stung her heart that the person she imagined growing old with could just fall out of love with her. Today, she finally wondered how she had ever been in love with him.

Sirens sounded in the distance. According to Brett, her phone had alerted the authorities. Help was on its way. She popped the trunk and heaved out her luggage, setting it in the grass. After gathering all of her personal belongings, she leaned against the car, waiting for someone to rescue her.

Alexa was struck by how green it was up north. As someone who had been born and raised in the biggest city in the United States, Central Park had been her idea of what a forest must look like. The mountain highways of New Hampshire proved her wrong. She felt like she was in the middle of nowhere, which, as inconvenient as that was at the moment, was a nice change of pace from her life in Manhattan. That was one of the big draws of Seasons Inn and a reason she could see suggesting that Gatton Investments buy it.

But standing alone on a deserted highway and only thinking about the other reason she had come all the way up here made her feel a little guilty. She was on vacation, *not* working. But… was it wrong that she could kill two birds with one stone—relax, and scope out a potential investment?

Alexa's best friend had recommended the inn to her, and if Melody knew she had decided to check it out for more than just a getaway, she'd be so disappointed. Melody had challenged her to prove that she could take a break from thinking about work for once. After all, that was one of Brett's reasons for wanting the divorce. He had accused her of being more married to her job than to him.

The sad truth was that work was more fulfilling than her marriage. It was where she felt the most competent, the place that she felt valued and needed. At home, she had never been enough. She didn't cook like Brett's mom. She had too many opinions. She wasn't funny anymore. She didn't want to quit her job and have a baby. Brett actually had the nerve to insinuate that not being ready to be a mom meant she wasn't going to be a very good one. That may have hurt more than all the other things he had said about her.

A lone police car made its way down the highway and slowed down as it approached the crash site. An officer jumped out and adjusted the hat on his head.

"Ma'am, are you all right? Anyone else with you?"

Alexa straightened. "I'm alone and uninjured, but the car isn't drivable."

"What happened?"

"One second, I was the only one on the road, and the next, there was a giant moose standing in the middle of the highway. I swerved to miss him and hit the tree instead."

He squinted and suspicion laced his words. "A moose? On the road? In the middle of a hot summer day?"

"Sure looked like a moose to me. It had a huge head and big antlers." She held her hands up on either side of her head and wiggled her fingers. "He took off as soon as I got out of the car."

"Can I get your license and registration?"

Alexa fumbled around her purse for her wallet. "I'm not going to get a ticket for getting in an accident because I was trying to avoid an accident, am I?"

"I'm going to have to make a report. You'll need one for your insurance," he replied as she presented him with her license. "Ah, New York. Where are you headed?"

"I'm vacationing at Seasons Inn for a few days."

"You were so close. It's just a couple miles up the road. Can I get the registration on the car?"

"It's a rental. Let me check the glove box." Alexa walked around to the passenger's side. A report wasn't the same as a ticket, she told herself. They couldn't fault her for what happened. It was unavoidable even if she hadn't been on her phone, which she was *not* going to mention.

"The Seasons Inn is real nice. I'm actually friends with the owners."

Alexa pulled out everything in the glove box and brought it over to the officer. Once he found what he needed, he went back to his car to write things up. An ambulance showed up and the EMTs checked her out, agreeing that it didn't seem like she needed medical attention.

"I can drop you off at the inn," the officer offered once he was finished. "Quinn or Nora should be able to get you a tow truck to take your rental to a shop in town."

Alexa sighed with relief. "Thank you."

A few minutes later, they pulled in front of the Seasons Inn, which sat up on a hill overlooking Lake Champney. The gorgeous Georgian-style architecture had been one of the things that attracted Alexa to this place when she'd looked it up online. The gray siding with the white trim and black shutters was simply stunning. Alexa was looking forward to the enclosed porch and all the cozy little spots tucked away for reading or relaxing. There were indoor and outdoor pools, as well as a beautiful flower garden out back.

Built for R & R, that was exactly how Alexa was going to use it.

"Thank you for the lift, Officer..."

"Lang. Name's Officer Jonah Lang," he said as he helped her get her bags out of his trunk.

"Well, thank you very much, Officer Lang."

"Hope the rest of your vacation goes a little bit better than how it started. Watch out for those daytime moose."

"I'll try to be more alert," she said, walking toward the entrance. She admired the leaded glass sidelights and transom surrounding the grand double doors. Her phone rang. Neil was finally checking on her.

"We got disconnected. I wanted to make sure everything was okay," he said when she answered.

"Almost hit a moose. I'm fine but my rental is not. Can you call the rental company and help me figure out what I need to do to get another car?"

"I'm on it."

The doors opened before her. Inside stood an older woman with a broad smile and a cheery disposition. She wore a pale blue polo shirt with Seasons Inn embroidered on the left side of her chest and a matching visor. Wild gray curls burst out of the top of the visor.

"Welcome to the Seasons Inn, where being

home away from home isn't just a saying but a reality. Oh! I didn't notice you were on the phone!" The woman pressed her lips together and then pretended to zip them shut, turn a lock, and throw away the key.

Alexa smiled in an attempt to ease the woman's mind. "Neil, I have to let you go. Let me know what you find out."

"I will." As if he knew she needed to know she was still needed, he reassured, "And, hey, we're going to be lost without you." His words were like a cool drink of water on a hot day, quenching that thirst Alexa had for positive affirmations.

She said goodbye to Neil and turned her attention to her greeter. "Thank you for the welcome. I'm here to check in."

"Stupendous! You head right over there to our front desk and I will get a cart for your baggage. My name is Maureen." She tapped on the name tag on the right side of her chest. "I'm here to help you with anything you need. They call me the bellhop, but I like to think of myself as the steward of a worry-free start to your vacation."

The bellhop was a woman who was definitely older than Alexa's mother. Never in a million years would Alexa allow her mother to get the bags. "I can get my things. You don't have to bother yourself with that."

"Bother? This is what they pay me to do, sweetheart." She ushered Alexa in and pointed her in the direction of the front desk. Maureen wasn't taking no for an answer.

Alexa stepped toward the front desk but was momentarily distracted by a man wearing a Seasons Inn T-shirt the same color as Maureen's polo and black athletic shorts. He strolled—in what seemed like slow motion—across the lobby. His arms were tan, as if he spent a lot of time outside doing push-ups, or whatever exercise would give him muscles that toned. He slid a hand through his golden brown hair as he grinned and gave a wink to another guest who passed him. There were dimples in his cheeks and he had a strong chin. Sunglasses dangled from a strap around his thick neck. Alexa had to shake her head to stop her flagrant gawking.

She gave him one last glance over her shoulder as he pulled Maureen in for a hug before exiting the inn. Hopefully, he wasn't leaving for good.

"Welcome to the Seasons Inn, how can I help you?" the man behind the desk asked. He was tall with the same golden brown hair as the other man. Instead of in his cheeks, he had a dimple in his chin. Where had Melody sent her? A place that only hired old women and gorgeous men?

"I'm here to check in. The reservation is under the name Fox. Alexa Fox."

"Ah, Mrs. Fox. We were expecting you." His assumption knocked her right out of her happy place.

"Ms. It's Ms. Fox," Alexa clarified, hating the way her new title sounded as much as she hated saying it. She had considered going back to her maiden name, but she was known in the business world as Alexa Fox. She didn't think she'd have the energy to explain to everyone who she was if she changed her name. Changing the title was bad enough.

The man's name tag read Quinn—one of the names Officer Lang had mentioned. "I apologize, Ms. Fox. We have been expecting you. You will be staying in our Garden Suite—"

"Oh," she interrupted him. "I didn't reserve a suite. I booked a basic guest room with a king-size bed."

"You did book a basic guest room," he said with a knowing smile. "A generous friend and former guest called and had you upgraded."

Melody. This was why the woman was her best friend in the entire world.

Quinn handed her the key to her suite.

Alexa remembered that she had a laundry list of things to do before she could relax. "Quinn, I just realized you are exactly who I am looking for. I was in a minor accident on the way up here. Officer Lang told me that you'd be able to help me get a tow truck for my car."

"Oh, I'm so sorry to hear that. I can get someone out there right away. Is there anything else I can help you with?"

"I am sure there is, but let's start with that."

He nodded and picked up the phone. Maureen appeared with a full cart. "I can deliver everything up to your room. That way you can take care of everything else."

This place was making quite the first impression. "Thank you so much. I'm in the Garden Suite."

"Ah, that has an amazing balcony that overlooks the gardens out back. You're going to love it." Maureen gave her a wink.

Alexa pulled out her phone and sent a quick text to Melody, promising to call her when she got to her *suite*. Her best friend sent back three heart emojis and the word *ENJOY* in all caps.

Quinn handed her the phone and she gave all the information to the tow-truck driver. Neil was handling the rental-car company. She needed to contact her insurance agent, but first, she wanted to check out this beautiful place. Glancing around the lobby, Alexa took in the charming atmosphere. There was a fireplace to the right with some oversize chairs covered in a buttery chenille. To the left was the front desk, where

Quinn was now helping another guest. The white wainscoting was the perfect contrast to the soft blue wallpaper.

"Welcome to the Seasons Inn. I'm Gavin Seasons, owner of this establishment. Can I help you find anything?" The man standing next to her was dressed in the familiar blue polo. Even though he was balding and there was a peppering of silver strands in what was left of his hair, it was clear he'd had the same golden brown hair as the two other workers in his younger days.

If Alexa was going to make the most of her time here, she was going to have to take advantage of everything that this place had to offer. Melody had assured her she could redefine herself on this trip if she wanted to. All she had to do was go for it.

"I think I'd like to talk to the concierge about the activities going on over the next few days."

Gavin's eyes lit up. "Well, let me introduce you to my daughter, Nora. She can get you signed up for a variety of activities and excursions." He led her over to a smaller desk near the spot where she checked in. "Nora, this is…"

"Alexa Fox."

"Ms. Fox would like to hear about all the exciting things we have planned here and around Apple Hollow," he continued. "I trust you will get her set up."

"You got it," the young woman replied with a dazzling smile. Her hair was a darker brown and she was much shorter than Alexa but shared an obvious resemblance to her father. She gave her full attention to Alexa. "Let's start with the things you enjoy doing and then I'll share some things perhaps you've never done before."

That should have been easy. Of course, Alexa was sure that they didn't have activities related to project management or business consultation. Her lack of interests outside of work was another one of those things that Brett had made her feel bad about.

"Can I be honest with you?"

Nora leaned closer. "Please."

"I don't know what I enjoy. I've spent the last decade trying to make a name for myself in my career. I accomplished that, but it cost me my marriage. I'm here to figure out how to be a more well-rounded person."

Nora's expression softened as sympathy oozed from every pore. "I hear you. This is what I'm going to do—I am going to put together the most amazing itinerary for you. It's going to be full of all the best things Apple Hollow has to offer, as well as the relaxation we provide here at the Seasons Inn." She placed a hand over Alexa's. "Come by tomorrow morning and I will have everything ready for you."

If everything went as planned, the Seasons Inn was about to offer her a chance to get a new perspective on life, as well as prove itself to be an outstanding addition to Roger's portfolio.

CHAPTER TWO

ONE THING WAS CERTAIN—Brady Seasons could always trust his sister to make his life more challenging than it needed to be.

"Okay, here are the lists for the day." Nora handed him the sheets with the names of guests signed up for today's events and excursions. "And I have a tiny favor to ask."

Nora's favors were never tiny.

"If you look on the paddleboarding tour sheet, you'll see two names with stars next to them."

Brady shuffled through the papers until he found the one she was talking about. There were handwritten stars next to the names Alexa Fox and Richard Leroy. Brady rubbed the back of his neck. "I'm not getting involved in your games, Nora."

"Please! You don't have to do anything except pair them up during the tour, give them a chance to get to know each other. Normal help-your-favorite-sister-out stuff."

Nora believed herself to be somewhat of a

matchmaker. For years, she'd been setting up everyone from her friends to coworkers. Not even guests were safe from her desire to play cupid. It didn't help that at least once a year someone claimed they met and fell in love at the Seasons Inn. Nora was always quick to take full credit for the happy couple. She also had no qualms about enlisting the help of anyone and everyone at the inn to make the love connections happen.

"Favorite or *only* sister?"

She placed a hand on his shoulder and gave him those sad-puppy eyes. "Both. Come on. We have a guest who is here alone. She needs some companionship."

He shrugged her off and shook his head. "How do you know that this...Alexa Fox and Richard Leroy will get along? Do people really come up to the concierge desk asking you to find them a date?"

"Mr. Leroy is the only single guy in a party of five visiting here for the week. Ms. Fox is recently divorced and vacationing solo. I have spoken to both of them and I think they're a perfect match for the time they're here. I need your help introducing them in a natural setting."

There was nothing natural about forcing two strangers to interact because his sister decided they would be perfect for each other, but Nora was so confident. Brady thought it was weird.

With a sigh and an eye roll, he gave in. "Fine. But if they don't get along, don't blame me."

"They will and they'll be able to thank me for the amazing time."

Brady chuckled. "If we actually calculated the amount of joy you and I bring to the lives of our guests, I think I would win by a landslide."

Nora's expression was incredulous. "That's hilarious. I don't think I have ever met a more delusional—"

Quinn suddenly appeared at Brady's side. "Let's not fight in front of the guests or I'm going to tell Mom and Dad on you two," he said in a quiet yet menacing singsongy voice.

Nora burst into laughter. "What are we? Children? You're going to tell on us?"

Brady folded his arms across his chest. "Is this a strategy you learned at that fancy leadership seminar Dad sent you to? There's no way tattling was something they taught you at manager school."

Quinn's mouth tightened into a grimace. "Get back to work. I'm serious."

Brady stepped back from the concierge desk and put his hands up in surrender. "Oh, I didn't realize he was serious. I'd better get back to work. You two have a blast standing at your desks all day while I go have some fun."

Without a doubt, Brady believed he had the

best job of the Seasons siblings. Every day was different. He got to be outside and participate in all the activities they had planned for their guests to enjoy. First, he had to check on the pool staff and make sure they had things under control. There was a pool party scheduled for later today and everything needed to be perfect.

He cut through the dining room so he could grab one of his mother's summer berry breakfast pastries. Laura Seasons was an incredible pastry chef and she shared her gift with all of the lucky guests of the inn. While their father took care of the operations side of things, their mom worked in the kitchen making delicious goodies to go along with breakfast, lunch, and dinner.

The dining room hummed with early morning conversations over coffee and the tinkling sound of silverware hitting plates. Brady could see the plate of pastries on the buffet table, his mouth watering at the thought of sinking his teeth into one. Out of nowhere, something small hit his face. Momentarily stunned, he froze in place. His eyes fell to the ground, where a green grape sat in front of him.

"I am so sorry!" A woman approached him, absolutely horrified. "I tried to poke a grape with my fork and instead of piercing it, it sent the thing flying through the air. Again, I am so sorry."

Brady bent over and picked up the apparently thick-skinned green globe, then chuckled. "That was one heck of a direct hit. I bet you couldn't do that again if you tried."

The woman pressed her hand to her chest and seemed unsure if she should laugh as well. Her skin was so pale compared to his. She was either a big fan of sunscreen or someone who did not spend much time outside, like he did.

"It's okay," he said, handing her the grape. "I wasn't injured by your reckless attempt at stabbing your fruit salad."

His good-natured teasing finally eased her tension. She had a lovely face when she smiled. Her long blond hair was pulled up into a ponytail and she had a tiny but noticeable mole on her right cheek. She was tall. He liked that he didn't have to look down to see into her eyes.

She took the grape from his hand. "I promise to be much more careful with my food moving forward."

"I trust you," he said with a wink. "Enjoy the rest of your breakfast."

The woman's gaze was locked on his and the two of them stood there for a moment longer than necessary. She looked like she wanted to say something. Her lips parted but no words came out. Brady noticed she had green eyes that were rimmed with blue. They reminded him of the color of the Atlantic off the coast of Maine.

"Are you okay?" he asked, wondering if she would speak again.

She shook her head, not in response to his question but more like she was clearing her thoughts. "I'm fine. Sorry again." She backed away and sat down at a table she didn't appear to be sharing with anyone else.

The inn had seen many guests come and go over the years. Brady had learned long ago not to get attached, but there was something about this woman that made him take one more look in her direction. It had been three months since his relationship with Sabrina, whom he'd been together with for over a year, had ended. Breakups were not fun, and Brady was trying to live a life with fun at the core. That meant relationships with strings were off the table. A little playful conversation with a pretty guest was safer than chatting up someone from town.

Brady grabbed his pastry and snuck out the doors to the patio on his way to the outdoor pool. Even though he loved skiing and snowboarding in the mountains during the winter months, summer was Brady's favorite season. He could spend the whole summer on the lake and never be bored—and that was just a taste of the fun to be had this time of year.

"Morning, Brady!" The pool attendant greeted his boss. Brady unlatched the gate to let himself in. Kayden was a seventeen-year-old who had practically grown up at the Seasons Inn. His mother, Alice, was the head of housekeeping.

"Morning. Just checking to make sure we're ready for this afternoon's pool party. Is there anything we need before I head out to the lake this morning?"

"We're golden. I don't—" Kayden began as he tripped over a pool toy. Like a fawn on ice, he nearly did the splits and ended up in a pose that made him look like he was playing a game of Twister. The boy was all arms and legs. He had grown a full four inches in one year and was still trying to figure out his new body.

Brady offered him a hand, trying hard not to laugh. "You good, man?"

Kayden straightened himself up and his cheeks bloomed red. "Yeah, I'm good. Everything's good. Ivy already had Wade drop off the tables she's getting Curt to load up with snacks."

Ivy was a huge help making this party a reality. She was the events manager, in charge of all the big and small events they threw at the inn. She and Brady crossed paths all the time since, as the activities director, he was in charge of planning and implementing a regular schedule of activities for guests. He was the one who led the adventure activities while Ivy was the one who set up and monitored the execution of the events. It sounded like she had already made sure the maintenance crew and kitchen staff were on top of things as well.

"Great, I will see you later when it's closer to party time. I've got to go get the paddleboards out of the shed."

It was a typical summer day at the inn. The sun was shining, and the guests were slowly rising from their relaxing evening slumber. Soon, the pool would be full of children and the lawn would be scattered with people taking a walk to the lake or exploring the garden, or maybe even playing some croquet or a game of giant chess.

Brady loved the Seasons Inn. In his opinion, it was one of the best places in the world. He was sure it had the potential to be the ultimate vacation destination in New England if marketed right. But whenever he had broached the subject with his dad in the past, his ideas came out as a scattered mess. Brady was more of a big-ideas guy than a write-a-business-plan kind of guy, which was why he stuck with keeping his focus on having fun and left the business planning to his older brother, Quinn.

Number one on his agenda was to get things ready for the first adventure of the day—a paddleboarding tour around the lake. Once he got the equipment out of the shed and down to the water, he headed back up to meet the guests on the list on his clipboard.

The outdoor patio was the meetup spot for all the lake adventures. Sometimes it was kayaking, other days it was canoeing. Today was paddleboarding day. It was one of Brady's favorites because, if he was honest, it was fun to watch the different learning curves. People new to paddleboarding inevitably fell in the water at least once. There was a reason entire internet vlogging channels were dedicated to people falling—it was funny. The coach in him also liked seeing those who struggled in the beginning get the hang of it and find out how enjoyable it could be.

He wasn't sure how experienced today's group would be, but he was about to find out. There was a small group gathered in the designated meeting spot. Brady checked his list. There were ten guests on it.

James and Cate Gilman and their two teenage children, Donovan and Kayleigh, chatted among themselves. Cate held her phone up and corralled the family in for a group selfie. Donovan stuck his tongue out and held up the peace sign much to his mother's dismay. The other group was made up of two couples and one single guy, whom Brady assumed was Richard Leroy. He was definitely the fifth wheel, scrolling through his phone as the couples chatted. The guy adjusted the baseball hat on his head, revealing the receding hairline that was hiding under there. Brady glanced around, wondering where Alexa Fox could be.

"Good morning," he said as he reached the group. "My name is Brady, and I am here to take you down to the lake for our paddleboarding tour."

Donovan raised his hand. "After the tour, can we paddleboard on our own for a bit?"

"Absolutely."

Cate's hand went up. "What if we have never done this before?"

Brady gave her a reassuring smile. "We're going to take some time in the beginning to make sure everyone gets the hang of it before we head out. I promise, I never leave anyone behind. I'm going to read off your names. Please let me know you're here and if you see yourself as a beginner, intermediate, or expert."

James and Cate were both beginners. Kayleigh went with being intermediate while her brother professed to be an expert. Everyone in Richard's group said they were intermediate.

"That leaves Alexa Fox," Brady said, ready to cross her name off the list. Too bad for Nora. There would be no love connection today if the woman failed to show up for the date she didn't know she was being set up on.

"I'm here! I'm here for the paddleboarding tour," someone called out breathlessly as if she had run from one side of the property to the other.

When Brady glanced up, his heart skipped a beat. It was the woman from breakfast. She had changed into her bathing suit and a bright pink cover-up. The flip-flops she wore had surely slowed her down as she had raced to the meetup spot.

"You have to tell him if you are a beginner, intermediate, or expert on a paddleboard," Donovan said, catching her up.

She gave him a grateful smile before turning her attention to Brady. She paused as if taking it in that the man she had hit with a grape this morning was leading her paddleboarding adventure.

"Um, I am definitely a beginner. I'm not even sure I know what a paddleboard is. Isn't it the little boat you sit in and use your feet to pedal like a bike?"

"That would be paddle-*boating*. We're going out on paddle*boards*. It's like a big surfboard that you stand on and you use a paddle to move you along," he explained, making the motion of pulling a paddle through the water.

Her eyes widened. "Oh, that makes sense," she replied.

Brady hoped Ms. Fox knew how to swim because something told him she was about to spend a bit of time in the lake today. He motioned for everyone to follow. "Let's head down to the water and practice on the boards before we take a tour around Lake Champney."

Being on the lake was one of Brady's favorite things to do. He loved taking guests out and showing them the fun they could have on the water. One of the ideas he wished his dad would hear him out on was using the lake to generate even more visitors to the inn. Brady imagined teaming up with other businesses in town and hosting events that would not only draw in more guests, but also give locals a reason to come to the Seasons Inn and spend a little money in the restaurant, or on some merchandise in their shop.

"If I am terrible at this, I don't want to hold up the whole group. I will happily go sit by the pool if this isn't for me," Ms. Fox said from behind him.

Brady slowed until she was walking beside him. "Are you asking me to give up on you before we even begin?"

Her lips twitched upward. "I am just letting you know that I would rather be told I can't go on the tour than ruin everyone else's time. Please. Don't let me be that person."

"You would have to have no ability to balance for me to give up on you."

"Okay, I think I have some balance." Immediately after those words left her mouth, she stumbled on an invisible trip hazard in the grass.

Brady reached for her arm to steady her. She grimaced before laughing. Her ability to laugh at herself was endearing. She had an infectious kind of giggle. Brady couldn't help but chuckle himself. "Well, I hope you don't mind getting wet because I think that's inevitable, but if you listen to my directions, you will get the hang of it and enjoy the lake tour. I haven't had to kick anyone off the water yet and I don't plan to start with you."

"I hope I don't make you second-guess yourself."

Brady let go of her and had to shake off the weird tingles she was giving him. She was a guest at the inn, not someone for him to flirt with. "I believe in you, Ms. Fox."

"Alexa. You can call me Alexa."

Brady smiled. "You've got it, Alexa." He liked the way her name sounded. He shook his head slightly and gave his neck a rub. *Guest, guest, guest*, he reminded himself.

Brady led his group down to the shed. The

shed was where they got their equipment and could lock up their personal belongings while they were on the tour. They were all encouraged to leave their phones onshore. Everyone on the tour also had to wear a bright orange life jacket for insurance purposes.

Brady, on the other hand, refused to get annoying tan lines. He had paddleboarded this lake more times than he could count. Not only did he forgo the life vest, but he also took off his Seasons Inn T-shirt. The way Alexa's eyes slid over his chest did not go unnoticed.

He assigned each person a board. The smartest thing he could do was remember his sister's plan to match Alexa up with Richard. Once the two of them hit it off, he could stop thinking about how nice her perfume smelled and how her eyes looked more blue than green outside compared to when he'd first seen them inside. *Guest, guest, guest.*

"We're going to pair off. Everyone needs a buddy out there. That way, if someone needs assistance, their buddy can call for my help. Looks like we have an even group here. Mr. Leroy, I was thinking you could pair up with Ms. Fox. Everyone else has a partner."

"Would it be okay if my cousins and I did a group of three?" Richard asked, refusing to budge from his place between his friends.

Nora had really picked a winner here. Brady put his hand on his hip. "I really need everyone to have a partner."

"I think there's a pool chair calling my name…" Alexa mumbled under her breath.

Brady shot her a look, and she quickly pressed her lips together.

Reluctantly, Richard moved over by Alexa. She stuck out her hand and he shook it as she apologized for the situation. "I promise that if I hold you back, I will quit and head for shore."

"Thanks," he replied. Brady was going to have a serious talk with Nora about her skills in finding someone a perfect match. This guy was about as far from anyone's ideal match as possible.

After a brief discussion about basic safety and handling of the board, Brady had them get in the water. He demonstrated getting on, starting on his knees. He explained that it was okay to take a few strokes like that before trying to stand.

"Then you're going to put the paddle in front of you like this and put your feet where your knees were." Brady stood up and pointed toward the opposite shore. "You want to make sure that you look up and out at something in the distance. You don't want to look down at the water or lean at the waist. That's the fastest way to lose your balance and fall in." Brady pushed his paddle through the water a couple of times. "Keep your chest up and hold your paddle like this."

Once he had shown them how to paddle, he spun himself around and invited everyone to get on their boards and give it a go. He watched as Donovan climbed on his board and was on his feet in seconds. His parents were a bit more tentative.

His sister, Kayleigh, used her paddle to splash him. "Show-off!"

The two teenagers began a water fight that rivaled some of the ones Brady had gotten into with his siblings when they were that age. He didn't have to intervene, though. Their parents put an end to their antics quickly by threatening to take away their phones for the rest of the vacation if they didn't stop.

Richard and his group all managed to get on their knees. Two of the men and one of the women began carefully getting to their feet. Brady noticed that Alexa was still standing next to her board, knee-deep in the water.

He paddled over to her. "I am definitely not letting you quit before you even try getting on the board."

Her sunglasses were perched on her head and she looked up at him with one eye shut. "I'm trying to decide if I should dunk myself now, so that when I fall in, which we both know I am going to do, it won't be as cold."

"Well, first, I would suggest that you let me hold on to these so they don't end up at the bottom of the lake." Brady crouched down and plucked her glasses off her head. "Then, I would say you need to have a tiny bit more faith in yourself. You might not get wet at all."

Alexa let out a breathy laugh as she shook her head. "You're funny. A terrible liar but so, so funny."

Almost everyone else was up on their feet. One of the men in Richard's group had one foot flat on the board and the other knee still firmly planted. He seemed to be stuck in that uncomfortable position.

"Just push up on that foot and get your other foot down," Brady suggested. "Use your arms to help you keep your balance."

The man tried to do as Brady said, but as soon as he tried to lift up, his body weight shifted and he began to sway from side to side. He lost hold of his paddle and down he went with a splash. His wife paddled over to him, having a hard time keeping a straight face.

"I knew you'd be the first one in, Ivan!" Richard teased. "I should have put some money on it!"

Brady tensed. If Richard said anything to Alexa, if...okay, probably *when* she fell in,

Brady was going to make sure he knew what it felt like to get wet as well.

He turned his attention back to Alexa. "Now, it seems the worst thing that can happen is that you're the second person to fall off. You've got this. Just get on your knees."

He watched as she took a deep breath and said something to herself too softly for him to make out. She placed one of her palms on the board and climbed on top. The way she beamed up at him with such a sense of accomplishment sent a burst of warmth right to the center of his chest.

"Good job. Paddle around like that for a minute. Get a feel for it."

Everyone else was practicing how to maneuver their boards. Ivan managed to get back on his and stood up with his wife's encouragement. Alexa was the only one left kneeling.

"What if I just tour the lake like this?" she asked. "I feel like I could get the same experience from down here. Why do I need to stand?"

"I don't want you to have any regrets," Brady said. "But if you think you'll be fine without even trying to stand on the board, then you're welcome to stay like that for the tour."

He could tell by the way she bit down on her bottom lip that Alexa was not usually one to shy away from a challenge. He could also tell that she wasn't someone who enjoyed failing, either.

The need to succeed and a fear of failure were battling it out inside her.

She took another deep breath and the lines in her forehead deepened. "I need to at least try."

Brady loved that answer. "You've got this," he insisted.

Alexa laid the paddle across the board and pressed her hands on top of it. She blew out a breath and carefully lifted up and placed one foot where her knee used to be. Just like poor Ivan, she was stuck in that position, scared to move.

"One more foot and you'll be standing tall. Look straight ahead. Don't look down at your feet or the board."

Her body shook and the board moved with it. She didn't give up. Alexa steadied herself and the board followed. She lifted off her knee and set down her other foot. On wobbly legs, she rose to her full height, her paddle held tightly in a death grip.

Brady had taken out numerous groups over the years. He had helped so many people figure it out, but had never felt so proud as when Alexa stood on her board, grinning from ear to ear.

"I told you you could do it!" he said with enthusiasm.

Their eyes met, and Brady felt a little knocked

off balance himself. He adjusted his stance. Alexa did not.

Her look of excitement quickly turned to horror as the board flew out from under her and she was met with the cool water of Lake Champney.

CHAPTER THREE

ALEXA WISHED SHE had dunked herself in the lake before getting on that board. The shock of the cold water was enough to take her breath away. It definitely wiped away whatever that wild feeling was that she had right before she lost her footing.

Was the hot, shirtless paddleboarding guy flirting with her? Of course not. He was doing his job. Surely, he'd been taught how to make his guests feel special. It didn't mean she really *was* special. He was just supposed to make her believe she was, and he was doing a really good job of it.

When she popped back up, she had garnered the attention of the entire group. Embarrassment heated her cheeks even though goose bumps covered her arms.

"Well, you got that over with. Lots of people fall in at least once." Brady was probably trying to make her feel better about it, but just as he said it, one of the other men in the group leaned forward, then back, and took a dive off his board.

There were a few chuckles from the group, but overall everyone seemed much more focused on staying upright on their own paddleboard than worrying about who was falling in. Maybe it wasn't such a big deal. Alexa pulled herself back on her board and rubbed her hand over the gooseflesh on her arm.

"Are you okay?" Brady asked once she was settled on her knees.

Alexa squeezed some water out of her ponytail. Other than wishing she was talking to him while not wearing a bright orange life jacket, there were no major problems. "I'm fine. I think I'll stay on my knees for a little bit."

His smile made her feel a bit gooey inside. "You do what feels best, but I believe that if you give yourself another chance, you'll master this thing in no time."

As much as she appreciated his faith in her, she planned on kneeling the rest of the tour. She paddled ahead, trying not to compare herself to the rest of the group, who were all on their feet.

"All right, let's make sure everyone is with their buddy," Brady said, paddling to the front of the group. He pointed to the east side of the lake. "We're going to head this way to Whispering Willow Cove. Follow me."

Alexa's reluctant buddy glanced back at her over his shoulder. "You're good, right?"

She gave him a thumbs-up and stayed in the back of the pack. There was no way she was going to force that guy to go at her pace no matter what the paddleboarding tour rules were.

The lake sparkled in the morning sun. It looked as if there were thousands of glittering lights dancing on the water. Alexa took a moment to appreciate how beautiful it was. The sights made up for the smells, which were mostly fishy but also peaty from the seaweed. She grabbed her ponytail and brought it to her nose for a sniff. Her floral shampoo had lost the fight the moment she hit the water.

This was a gorgeous location for the inn. Her business mind kicked in as she thought of all the ways she could sell the idea of taking over the place to Roger. She shivered as a breeze brushed against her wet skin just as the guilt of focusing on work instead of relaxation hit her like a ton of bricks. Brett would have complained about how distracted she was by work. So distracted that she had failed to keep up with the group. They were nowhere to be seen. Alexa began paddling in the direction she had last seen them.

This side of Lake Champney was edged in tall grasses and trees with slim trunks and broad leaves. The other side was peppered with houses and boat docks. It was quiet this time of day. The only other people on the lake seemed to be fishermen in boats with tiny trolling motors. How could she have lost the whole group?

Brady came flying out of a bend to the right. He used his paddle to slow down. "There you are! Your buddy really blew it. Are you okay? Did you fall in again?"

His concern was endearing, even more so because he was wearing his sunglasses, with hers perched on top of his head. "I'm fine. I stopped paddling to take in the view. The lake is so pretty, I had to take it all in. Sorry, I didn't mean to lose you guys."

"Don't apologize. Your buddy should have stayed close so that didn't happen." For some reason he seemed much more frustrated with her paddleboard buddy than she was. "I'm glad you're okay. We're not too far. The cove entrance is right over here."

"Can I get my sunglasses back? I feel like I'm not very likely to fall in from this position."

He paddled closer to her and handed them over. Alexa envied how easily he balanced on the board. He made it look so simple when she knew it was not.

She followed him while appreciating a different view. This time, she was focused on Brady's strong legs and the way his back muscles flexed as he paddled. His skin was such a perfect shade of golden brown that she thought he must have bribed the sun gods.

"I think I'll be your buddy for the remainder of the tour. Can you stay close?" he asked before they reached the rest of the group.

He wanted her to keep up with him? Alexa couldn't stop the giggle that bubbled out of her.

He tilted his head. "What's so funny?"

"I don't think there's any chance that I can stay close to you unless you paddle like you've never seen water before, and I'm not sure that's the pace the group is hoping for."

It was Brady's turn to laugh. "Like I've never seen water," he repeated with a shake of his head. "Well, I think you can do more than *you* think you can. I have a feeling that if you put your mind to it, you are the type of person who can do anything."

Alexa wanted to bathe in his words. They felt rejuvenating to that part of her psyche that took such a beating in the divorce. She was the type of person who didn't back down from a challenge, and she was also the kind of person who persevered when things got tough. She could do this if she focused and followed his lead.

"You're right. I will be right behind you the rest of the tour."

"That's the spirit." His smile was broad, and

she had to remember that he was trained to be hospitable. That megawatt grin was designed to make her feel good about her stay. It was not personal.

Once they caught up to the rest of the touring group, Brady quickly went into the history of Lake Champney and how it was named after a 19th century artist who helped make the White Mountains of New Hampshire famous. Whispering Willow Cove was featured in one of Champney's paintings. There was quite a picturesque group of willow trees lining the shore. Alexa could imagine one might be inspired to memorialize the view.

Staying close to the tour guide forced her to pay attention to what he was saying. Brady was full of fun facts and interesting historical anecdotes. When they arrived back where they had started, Alexa was disappointed it was over.

"I hope you all enjoyed our trip around the lake. Be sure to check with the concierge and find out what other adventures you can join me on during the rest of your stay."

Alexa unlatched the buckle on her life jacket before slipping it off. She had left the planning of her activities to the concierge. Hopefully, one of them would allow her to cross paths with the handsome Brady before her time was up.

"If you're looking for something to do later

today, don't forget about the pool party. I promise it's going to be worth your time," he announced to the group as they lined up to turn in their life jackets and pick up their personal belongings.

"Will there be a DJ?" Donovan asked. Alexa had noticed that the teenager had hummed to himself as they paddled around the lake.

"What kind of party doesn't have music?" Brady replied. "I don't know that I can call Kayden a DJ, but my aquatics assistant is very good at managing the playlist I chose."

Donovan frowned. "So it's going to be old people's music?"

His mother swatted him in the chest with the back of her hand, her eyes wide with parental secondhand embarrassment.

Brady took the dig like a champ. "I may be older than you, my friend, but that just makes me wiser about what qualifies as good music. Don't you worry."

Donovan's mom apologized for him and promised they would be at the pool party. Alexa was next in line and held out her life jacket, which actually had dried after that earlier unfortunate fall into the water.

"Can I count on you being at my pool party later today?" he asked her directly.

He was just being nice because that was what

he was supposed to do. His job was to get guests to come to the party. He wasn't asking because he truly wanted her specifically to be there.

"I didn't realize it was *your* pool party. That might change things for me. I have spent a considerable amount of time following you around already today."

His eyes crinkled in the corners as he narrowed them and smiled. "Oh, come on, you know you had the most fun when you were my buddy."

"Right. It was just like when no one wanted to be my partner in PE for the social dance section and I had to dance with the teacher, Ms. Gilmore. Not embarrassing at all."

Brady's mouth fell open. "Stop. It was not that bad, was it?"

Alexa laughed to let him off the hook. "It was not bad at all. Thank you for making sure I made it through the whole tour."

"My pleasure," he said with a tiny bow. "Now, tell me you'll be at the pool party."

Alexa shrugged, trying not to give it away that she had already planned to be there the second he mentioned it. "I'm not sure what my activity planner has on my schedule next, but if it says pool party, I'll be there."

"My sister would never want anyone to miss the pool party. It's on there," he said assuredly.

Brady was definitely never one of those kids who didn't get chosen to be someone's partner. In fact, he was probably the guy everyone prayed would choose them.

"Then I guess I'll see you later."

"I guess you will." He didn't even attempt to conceal his smirk. He was a flirt, and it had been a long time since someone purposely flirted with Alexa. Even if it was simply part of his job, she was going to enjoy it.

Alexa walked over to the picnic table to organize her stuff. She slipped her cover-up over her head and her flip-flops on her feet. She was going to text Melody as soon as she got back to her suite. Melody had to have met Brady during her visit.

"Someone looks like they had a good time paddleboarding," Nora said as Alexa made her way through the lobby.

"It was fun, and I only fell in once. Thankfully, it wasn't as embarrassing as I thought it would be."

"Well, hopefully you met some nice people." She looked at her expectantly. "Made some friends?"

Alexa wasn't sure she'd refer to anyone on the tour as her new friend. Most of them were very nice but probably weren't looking for a bestie on their week's vacation. Of course, there was Brady. She enjoyed his company most of all.

"Everyone seemed to have fun together. Brady was very good at keeping us all entertained."

"My brother can't get enough of being on the lake. His goal in life is to make everyone else love it as much as he does."

Alexa smiled at the memory of the pure joy on his face as he talked about the way the sunlight on the lake changed colors throughout the day, and how he couldn't even pick a favorite time of day because it was always so breathtaking. "He seemed to be trying very hard to win us land-lovers over."

Nora's eyebrows pinched together for a second, as if she was attempting to silently solve some problem. Alexa took that as her cue to move on.

"Don't forget about the pool party after lunch," Nora called after her. "Some of the other guests who went paddleboarding should be there. You can reconnect on solid ground this time."

Reconnecting with anyone from the tour group seemed like a strange thing to do, but Alexa humored her with a nod. When she got up to her suite, she fell onto her bed and texted Melody about her first morning at the inn. Instead of texting back, Alexa's phone rang with a call from her friend.

"Day one and you've already done your first

excursion and met Brady?" Melody giggled, just like she did when they used to talk on the phone about boys when they were in high school.

"You really set me up with lots of pretty things to look at, Mel."

There was more giggling. "And you're not just talking about the lake, are you?"

"You're terrible. I can't spend my whole vacation going gaga over some guy who works here. I'm supposed to be figuring myself out."

"Why can't you figure yourself out and enjoy the cute guys who work there? You're single and free to go gaga over whoever you'd like."

Alexa let out a sigh. "I hate being single. I am not mentally prepared for it. I should just plan on being alone the rest of my life so I don't make a fool of myself."

"Why would you make a fool of yourself? I'm not telling you to date the activities director. I'm giving you permission to look and flirt. These are low-risk activities, Lex."

"Flirting is not low-risk." Alexa rolled onto her side. "I haven't flirted with a man in years. Heck, in over a decade! I also have to constantly remind myself that not every man being nice to me is flirting with me. That's how I'm going to make a fool of myself—by flirting with someone who I think is flirting with me but isn't."

Melody clicked her tongue. "Flirting is like

riding a bike. You just need to get back on and give it a go. You'll be surprised how easily it comes back to you."

"I think I'd rather sit by the pool and read a book, or listen to all the true-crime podcasts that you recommended to me over the last year that I haven't made time for until now." She left out that she also wanted to do some snooping around to get some more information about the inn for Roger. She opened her email on her phone and scrolled through the new ones that had come in while she was on the water.

"That actually sounds like a dream vacation. I'm very happy to hear that you plan on doing exactly what you said you were going to do— take a real break from work and do something fun. Even if that doesn't include flirting with cute men."

Alexa closed her mail app as if Melody might be able to tell she was on it if she stayed on it too long. "No work. Just play," she lied. "That's my motto for the entirety of this trip."

A high-pitched scream came from the other end of the line and then another. "Ugh, I have to go before my daughters cause me to do something that will land me a starring role on one of those true-crime podcasts."

"Please don't do that," Alexa said with a chuckle.

"Take care and have fun. And don't be so afraid to be a little flirty." More screaming in the background and Melody turned her attention to her fighting children. "If you two don't stop it, I swear— Bye, Lex. Gotta go."

"Bye," Alexa replied before the call ended. Melody and her husband had three children, all two years apart. Two girls and one boy. There were times she envied her friend and then there were times like this that she was happy to be on the quiet end of the call once it ended.

If Brett had heard her thoughts, he would once again accuse her of being selfish. Being a parent was a blessing. She should *want* a family. His parents had had all four of their kids by the time they were thirty. Why was anything more important than being a mother?

Maybe there was something wrong with her. She was thirty-three and still not ready. Of course, having children was going to be a lot more difficult now that she wasn't married and there was no one to start a family with. What if the desire to be a mom kicked in now that she was alone? Brett would say that was the price she would pay for caring more about her career than a family.

Alexa sat up. She didn't want to think about the kids she might never have or how Brett made her feel. She needed to freshen up and get some lunch before checking out the pool party. There was no telling what that was going to entail. But if all that came from it was that she got to see Brady again, that was enough for now.

She managed to make it through lunch without sending any of her food flying from her plate. Then, just inside the pool area, she checked out a towel from a teenager in the cabana whose name tag read Kayden.

"Enjoy the party," he said as he handed her the towel.

She smiled in return and took a second to take in her surroundings. Kids of all ages were splashing and playing in the water. One boy adjusted his goggles, then shouted at his mom to watch him do a handstand. A couple was sitting on the edge of the pool sipping drinks and talking close. She followed the wet footprint marks on the stamped concrete to the loungers. There were several families and couples who had already staked their claim on seats. This was the one time it wasn't so bad being alone. One chair was much easier to find than two.

A whistle blew and a suntanned lifeguard shouted at some kids to not put their hands on each other. Alexa recognized Cate and James from the paddleboarding excursion. Their daughter was sunbathing on the chaise next to them as they stayed in the shade of an umbrella.

The screeching of a speaker caught her attention and someone tapped on a microphone. There, in the corner by tables full of snacks, was Mr. Brady Seasons in all his shirtless glory.

"Can you guys hear me?" he asked, speaking into the microphone. Some of the guests shouted yes. "Great. We're just about to get started. We have a fun couple of hours planned. We're going to get some music going and our first pool game will begin in five minutes. Please, help yourself to some of our goodies up here. Remember, no food in the pool, but you're more than welcome to enjoy any of these snacks on the pool deck. Thanks!"

Alexa found an open spot near James and Cate and set her beach bag down next to it. *Reconnect with the friends you made this morning*, Nora's voice said in her head. She unfolded her towel and carefully laid it on the chaise lounge.

Cate looked up from her book and recognized her. She smiled and raised a hand to say hello.

"Reading anything good?" Alexa asked, pulling a book from her own bag.

Cate set her bookmark in place. "My friends all read this in their book club and told me I had to read it. I'm not sure I'm a fantasy girl, though. It's about faeries and dragons. I don't know. Supposedly, there's a romance to die for in here somewhere."

Alexa hadn't heard of the book. "Romance and fantasy are pretty much the same thing to me these days. I prefer to stick to biographies and memoirs. Reality is always more twisted than fiction."

"Ain't that the truth!" Cate laughed.

The temperature had gone up quite significantly since they were on the water. Alexa's chair was not shaded like James's and Cate's. She tucked some hair behind her ear. She had brushed it out and put a hat on to come to the pool, but that wasn't going to be enough to keep her cool. A dip in the pool might help if she had any hope of comfortably doing some reading and watching the fun and games.

She set her book on her towel and shrugged out of her cover-up. As she adjusted her bathing suit, she noticed Brady staring right at her. It was comical that she had thought the sun was the only thing that could make her sweat. This eye contact with Brady caused her heart to race and her skin to feel like it was on fire. He waved and she reflexively did the same. Just as Melody had brought back those memories from high school, Brady made Alexa feel half her age. Except back in high school, boys like Brady didn't wave at her from across the pool.

Giddiness wasn't the only high-school feeling that reemerged. Standing there in her bathing suit, she suddenly felt extremely self-conscious. Alexa carried around more than a few pounds compared to her teenage self. Her thighs touched and her belly was nowhere near flat. She'd always been too tall compared to all the other girls. She hadn't worn heels in forever for fear that she'd be seen as some kind of giant. She needed to get in the water so there was no chance Brady or any other man at the pool had time to take in all her flaws.

Maybe it was because she was distracted by her insecurities, maybe it was simply her bad luck, but as she made her way to the side of the pool with the zero entry, a little boy scurried past her. As she twisted out of his way, an older boy barreled into her. It was an instant flashback to being on the paddleboard. She knew she was losing her balance, and just like this morning, she was underwater before she had any chance to regain it.

CHAPTER FOUR

BRADY SAW IT coming before she did. Some kid was chasing his little brother and knocked into Alexa, sending her flailing into the pool. He found himself kicking off his sandals and jumping into the water to make sure she was okay.

The hat that she had been wearing was now floating to the other side of the pool. He swam into the deep end and rescued it for her.

She stood in waist-high water and wiped her eyes. The kid who had knocked her in got an earful from his mother. She marched him over to the edge of the pool to apologize.

"Sorry," he mumbled.

Alexa was too gracious. "It's okay. I should have been watching where I was going."

"*He* should have been watching where he was going. We are so, so sorry," the mother said, nudging her son. "Right?"

"It was Benny's fault," the kid protested. "I was trying to stop him from running. I wouldn't have bumped into her if he hadn't almost run her over."

Brady had to hold back his laughter. The kid sounded exactly like Brady's older brother. Any wrongdoing had always been Brady's fault. Quinn would claim he had only been trying to stop Brady from doing whatever was really the problem. Brady could admit as an adult that sometimes that was true.

"It's really okay. Thank you for apologizing. I appreciate it," Alexa said. Satisfied, the mom and her son went back to their loungers.

Brady came up behind Alexa. "You know, the belly-flop contest starts at two o'clock. I think with a little more practice, you could do well," he joked as he placed the hat back on her head.

She covered her face with her hands. "Oh, my gosh, no one needs to see me fall in the water any more today. In fact, I think I'd better just stay in my room the rest of this trip."

"Stop it." He splashed some water playfully in her direction. "You were planning to get in the water, anyway, right? Everyone has moved on. Look," he said, motioning to the crowd, who had all gone back to their own business like nothing had happened.

Alexa cautiously dropped her hands and glanced around. Once she seemed sure no one was paying her any attention, she touched the top of her head and searched around her. "My sunglasses must have fallen off. They have to be here somewhere."

Brady went to work helping her retrieve them. He found them at the bottom of the pool, not too far from where she had surfaced a minute ago.

"Always coming to my rescue," she said.

"That's what I'm here for." All joking aside, he wanted to be sure she hadn't let that kid off the hook too easily. He touched her shoulder. "Are you sure you're okay?"

Her eyes flickered to his hand, which he snatched away immediately. He was an employee at the inn. He shouldn't be touching the guests.

She slid on her sunglasses. "I'm mortified, but fine. Definitely cooled me off." She pressed the back of her hands to her cheeks, flush with embarrassment. She was beautiful but somehow even more so when she was a little flustered.

"I hope things turn around and you have fun at the pool party. This thing was all my idea, so I want to make sure everyone has a good time."

Her eyebrows lifted above the rims of her sunglasses. "You're the party planner and the activities director?"

"Well, we have an event planner, but I like to throw a party or two sometimes. Parties can be a kind of activity, can't they?"

"I suppose so. You must be one of those multi-talented guys. You can paddleboard, play any sport, plan parties. You probably jump out of planes."

"Jump out of planes?" He cocked his head. "Where did that one come from?"

She gave him a crooked smile, her lips upturned on the side with that little mole. "I don't know. You give off that James Bond vibe, like one minute you could be waterskiing and the next you could be dressed to kill, mixing martinis before you have to parachute off a bridge or something."

"What?" He scrunched up his nose. She amused him with the way she thought.

Her cheeks were bright red. "I'm going to stop talking and go sit down and read a book because clearly I am so weird."

She moved around him to get to the ladder on the side of the pool. He followed her, trying really hard to control his gaze and not stare at how good she looked in a bathing suit. Now out of the water, she turned toward him. Her blond hair looked so much darker when it was wet.

"You are not weird," he said. "You are very fun to talk to, actually."

"I bet you say that to all the weird guests."

"Only the pretty ones." As soon as he said it, he knew he should be careful. Quinn would be signing him up for a professional-behavior course if he heard Brady talking to a guest like that.

Alexa let out a breathy chuckle, and she glanced down and away. "Thanks. For the compliment and for retrieving my hat and sunglasses."

"No problem." He had made it awkward. Mentally, he chastised himself as he made his way over to the cabana where Kayden was passing out towels.

"I'm going to get someone to cover for you so you can be in charge of the music and help Ivy hand out prizes when we get to the contests," Brady told Kayden, refocusing his attention on the tasks at hand. Engaging with guests about how pretty they were was not one of them.

"You got it, boss."

"How are things going?" His dad's voice caught his attention. Quinn and their dad entered the pool area wearing matching Seasons Inn polo shirts and khaki shorts.

"Where is your shirt?" Quinn questioned with his new managerial tone. "And why are you soaking wet? You know you're working. This isn't playtime."

"I was actually helping a guest who fell in the pool, thank you very much." Not that he had been wearing a shirt before that. He would not be cursed with a farmer's tan if he could help it.

"Is the guest okay? Did you fill out an accident report?"

Brady patted Quinn on the shoulder. His brother needed to relax. "It wasn't that serious. Everyone is A-OK."

"Is there anything I can do to help with the party?" his dad asked.

"You didn't send out the agenda or give anyone a heads-up about what they could do to help," Quinn quickly added. Given his constant criticism, Brady had to wonder if Quinn's whole purpose in life was to point out all the ways Brady did things differently.

"Ivy and I have everything worked out." As if on cue, Ivy announced it was time for the first game—water volleyball. "I didn't give the family tasks because I didn't need you to do anything."

His dad clapped his hands together. "Great! Then I can walk around and visit with the guests."

While he went to do that, Quinn adjusted the collar on his shirt. "When we have an event like this, it's best to include at least Dad. As the owner of Seasons Inn, it's important for him to interact with guests when they are enjoying themselves the most. If you would have sent me an agenda, I could have given you that feedback earlier."

Brady didn't write up agendas. He was the one who knew how to have fun and help everyone else do the same. Agendas meant sitting in front of a computer and typing a bunch of words into an email. Brady had chosen to be activities director to avoid ever sitting behind a computer.

"You see me every day, Quinn. All you have to do is ask me and I'll tell you. I don't know why you need everything in an email."

"Because that's how a successful business is run. Something as simple as sending an email can help keep everyone on the same page."

"I'll be sure to remember that for the next pool party," Brady said, wanting nothing but for this conversation to be over. One of the pool attendants walked by and Brady stopped her. "I need you to take over for Kayden at the towel cabana so he can help Ivy."

The girl nodded and did as she was instructed. Quinn surveyed the pool and pool deck. "I guess you have everything under control. I'm going to take care of other business then."

Brady stopped himself from saying something snotty and gave a little wave goodbye instead. He loved his brother, but he wasn't the easiest person to work with, family or not. Brady did a scan of the pool deck. His dad chatting with Alexa gave him pause. She laughed at something he said. His dad was a charming guy and the ultimate host. His mother often said the man was born to run this inn.

Brady was drawn to them, needing to know what was being said. As he got closer, he heard his dad sharing how much acreage they owned.

"Have you ever considered expanding or opening another location?" Alexa asked.

"I have my hands full with this place. I can't imagine having more to manage. I'm an old man, if you haven't noticed. I'll leave big changes to my kids when they take over."

"Well, you know there are a lot of people out there who could help with things like expansion and franchising. You wouldn't have to do it on your own."

"Oh, I know there are. I think what makes this place special is that it's family-run, family-owned. You know you're going to be treated differently because it's like we're inviting you into our home. It's not just a business."

"Your kids feel the same way? About keeping it in the family?"

"I think so," his dad answered.

"We all want to keep it in the family," Brady interrupted. "How else am I going to be able to throw a lake party instead of a pool party next summer?"

Alexa shifted her gaze. Brady could still picture the green in her eyes even though they were currently concealed by those sunglasses. "You mean a beach party?" she asked with a smirk.

"Nope, the party I imagine throwing is on the lake *and* the beach. It's gotta be called a lake party."

"You never do anything halfway. Am I right?"

Brady liked that she already understood his personality. "Dead on."

"Ms. Fox had nothing but nice things to say about you when we first started talking," his dad revealed. "Sounds like your paddleboarding excursion was a hit."

"It always is."

Alexa still seemed amused by him. Brady decided amused looked even better on her than flustered. "Did I mention that his confidence is endearing?" she asked his dad.

"My son is and always has been full of confidence and more energy than you could think possible. The combination makes him very... What's the right word?"

"Entertaining?" Brady offered.

"Let's go with that," his dad said.

"Highly entertaining," Alexa added.

Brady wanted to show her everything the inn and the town had to offer. If entertainment was appealing, he could entertain her all day long. "Hopefully, Nora scheduled Ms. Fox to join me on Monday for the ATV trip so she can experience more of that endearing confidence and never-ending energy."

"You run the off-site activities, too?"

"I run all the activities. I thought we established that in our earlier conversation."

"ATV and four-wheeling are the same thing, right?"

It was oddly satisfying to know that he was getting to see her experience these things he loved for the first time. She had no idea all the fun she was about to have. "They are."

"Then you're stuck with me again."

That made him happier than it should have. "Excellent. I promise there's no water for you to fall in while we're out on the trails. We try hard to keep the ATVs out of water."

She clearly fought back a smile. "Good to know. Tomorrow I'm scheduled at the spa. That's not one of your activities, correct?"

"I am not involved with anything that happens at the spa. Sundays also happen to be my only day off."

Alexa frowned. "Bummer. For the guests, not you. I'm sure you enjoy having a day off."

Brady enjoyed the fact that she was disappointed he wasn't going to be around tomorrow. He probably shouldn't enjoy that as much as he did.

His dad cleared his throat. "Well, we'll let you

get back to your book. I am so happy to hear you have been enjoying your stay here so far. I hope that continues, Ms. Fox."

"Thank you, Mr. Seasons."

Brady followed his dad back to the pool entrance. "Looks like the pool party is off to a good start."

Brady couldn't disagree. The sounds of the volleyball players' laughter and water splashing filled the air. Guests were snacking on bags of chips and his mom's chocolate-chip cookies. Some teenagers were recording themselves dancing to the song playing. He saw lots of smiles and plenty of fun being had.

"It's just like I imagined it."

His dad pulled a handkerchief from his pocket and wiped the sweat beading on his forehead. It was warm but not that warm. Brady noticed how red his dad's face was.

"Are you okay? You look like you're overheating. Let me grab you some water." He ran over to the snack table and dug out an ice-cold water bottle from one of the buckets. He jogged back to his dad. "Here, drink some of this. Mom won't like it if you get heatstroke."

"I'm fine," he said, uncapping the bottle and taking a swig. "You've done a good job with the party, son."

The compliment hit Brady in the center of his

chest. He often sought his father's approval but was usually overshadowed by Quinn and his business-school degree.

"Maybe we can talk about my ideas for a lake party. I think—"

His dad held up a hand to stop him. "We've talked about this, Brady. I love your ideas, but too many times we talk about them and then I never see the who, what, when, where, and how much. I can't sign off on something that's simply spinning around in that head of yours. Put it on paper and then we'll talk about it."

It didn't matter that he was able to pull off this pool party with nothing more than the ideas that had been "spinning around in his head" and Ivy. She was better at handling logistical issues than he was. As soon as he had told her what he wanted to do for the pool party, she knew exactly how many tables and what other equipment they needed to have on hand. Maybe she could help him write this proposal that his dad needed to hear him out.

"And I know that your mother would tell me you're just like me, but make sure your charm doesn't cross the line when it comes to the guests."

He didn't have to name names for Brady to know who he was talking about. He was enjoying the banter with Alexa more than he should. She was a guest here for a few days.

He saluted his dad to show him he would follow orders. Keep it professional, he told himself. He could do that. He would.

After the pool party ended with everyone having a good time, Brady made his way to the lobby to check out with Nora for the day. She made him return his lists and give her some feedback on who should or should not have participated in each activity that day.

"I heard the pool party was a good time," she said as he approached.

"If Kayden posts the video of the belly-flop contest, we're going to go viral for sure." He handed her the guest lists from his activities. The paddleboarding tour and the pool party had both gone well. He had no concerns about anyone who participated.

"How did Ms. Fox and Mr. Leroy get along during paddleboarding? Did they hit it off? Were they hanging out at the pool party? I encouraged her to connect with her new 'friends' while she was there."

"I think you might have missed the mark on that one, sis. Mr. Leroy ain't it. He's a thumbs-down for Alexa."

"A thumbs-down for *Alexa*?"

"Ms. Fox. Whatever you want to call her. She asked me to call her Alexa, so I did."

Nora was visibly frustrated. "Did you even partner them up?"

"I tried. He wanted nothing to do with her. He only wanted to hang out with the people he's here with. He didn't care about being a fifth wheel. He loved fifth-wheeling."

"Well, he's going *four*-wheeling on Monday and so is Alexa. It's only the six of them. Let's give them another chance. He stopped by the desk and told me how much fun he had paddleboarding this morning. I thought that it was because of the lovely lady he was paired with." She frowned. "Maybe he's shy. He needs another shot at connecting with her. Was she friendly? Did she try talking to him?"

Brady's shoulders fell as he sighed. Nora was delusional. To her credit, several people she'd supposedly schemed to pair up actually did end up falling in love, but she was not hitting the mark on this one. "Alexa is very friendly. She's funny and down-to-earth. There was nothing not to love. He showed her zero interest. I don't think he's looking for a love connection."

Nora shook her head. "I'm right about this. We're going to give it another chance."

The last thing he wanted to do was try to push Alexa on Richard Leroy. The guy was not right for her. She deserved someone who wanted nothing more than to give her attention, to listen to her talk about all the funny little thoughts in her head.

"I think you should let the woman enjoy her vacation without your meddling."

"I wonder if I can convince Mr. Leroy to sign up at the spa tomorrow."

"Nora," Brady said in a warning tone.

"What? Alexa Fox is going to get a taste of some romance during her stay here. I'm determined, and you know what happens when I'm determined."

Brady knew all too well, and for some reason he didn't like the thought of someone romancing Alexa one bit. He shook his head, hoping to dislodge these thoughts of her. He had promised his dad he would keep things on the up-and-up. Professional. It was a good thing he had the day off on Sunday. If he had to watch Nora trying to push those two together, he wasn't sure he could fulfill that promise.

CHAPTER FIVE

Four-wheeling was less intimidating than paddleboarding. Alexa knew how to drive a car and could ride a bike fairly well. This machine was sort of a combination of a car and a motorbike. It had handlebars but also four wheels, making it feel much more stable. There would be no falling today. Not in water or on the ground.

"Does anyone have any questions?" Brady asked after going over all the basics.

Like Alexa, everyone else seemed comfortable with what they were doing. This was a smaller group than Saturday. The two couples and her former paddleboarding buddy were the only other guests on this excursion. Once again, Brady encouraged everyone to pair up with someone so no one got left behind. Since all of Richard's friends were couples, she was once again forced to partner up with him.

"You're going to try to keep up with the group today, right?" he asked.

Such a sweet guy. She couldn't understand

why he was single! "I plan to be at the front of the group. Hopefully, you can keep up," she said with a wink.

He didn't seem to know if he should take her seriously or not. He gave her a thumbs-up and put on his helmet. Alexa chuckled to herself. This was going to be fun. They were going to be on big, loud machines. She was thankfully not going to have to make small talk with this guy.

"Everyone get your helmet on. Anyone having any issues with the fit?" Brady asked, walking down the line.

Alexa put on her helmet but the straps wouldn't click together. She took it off and inspected the fasteners.

"Everything okay?" Brady stopped in front of her.

"I need to get a new helmet. This one is broken. These won't click together." She handed him her helmet and he tried to get it to work without any success.

"Yeah, this is no good. Hold on a second. I have a better idea than trading this one in." He jogged over to his fancy four-wheeler. It was a two-seater and his personal vehicle, which he said he had trailered up there earlier this morning. He came back with a white helmet. "All the buckles work on this one."

She put it on and he reached over and pressed

a button on the side of the helmet above her ear. His proximity made her feel a bit weak in the knees. He was fully clothed today, but somehow looked just as attractive in his long-sleeved T-shirt and khaki pants as he did in his swim trunks.

He stepped back, put on his helmet, and pressed a similar button on the side of his helmet. Suddenly, his voice was in her ear. "I'm letting you borrow my extra helmet. It has a built-in radio inside that's paired with mine so we can chat. You know, in case you get left behind by your buddy and need me to come get you."

She laughed. "Hey now, don't try to get between me and Richard. I think I'm starting to grow on him. He might even stay within a hundred yards of me today."

Brady's chuckle through the radio made her heart happy. "Yeah, we'll see about that."

He showed her how to turn the volume up and down, and warned her that she might have to listen to his favorite playlist while they rode.

"What kind of music do you listen to?"

"You'll have to wait to find out." She could hear the smile in his voice even though his face was covered by the helmet.

She had missed seeing him yesterday, although the spa had been a nice distraction. She had treated herself to the works and her body had never felt so relaxed. Her mind was another story. There had been a jumble of thoughts plaguing her. Between worrying about what she would be missing at work this week and taking some more notes on the inner workings of the inn, she somehow still found time to wonder what Brady did on his day off. Was he off having adventures on his own? Did he hang out with friends? Were any of those friends a girlfriend?

It was foolish to put so much thought into what was going on in someone's life when that someone was simply a temporary person in her life. A week from now, she'd be back in Manhattan.

Brady signaled for everyone to get on their machines and start their engines. Alexa didn't know what to expect, but the idea of riding with Brady in her ear, narrating her ride, made her giddy. Everyone had been given maps, but the idea was to stay together. They planned to make various stops along the trail for some sightseeing. With Brady in the lead, they were off.

The ATV was loud as it rumbled along the rocky trail. The path was lined with trees full of broad, green leaves. There would be no listening to birds chirping or water running over the rocks in the streams they passed, but there would be a friendly voice.

"So these trails cover about seventy-four hundred acres of land. They're open to ATVs in the warmer weather months and when there's snow, people can rent snowmobiles," Brady said through the built-in headset.

"I bet you have your own snowmobile, too."

"Of course I do. I actually like it better than this. It's a much smoother ride," he said as they came to a bouncy part of the trail.

"I think my butt would appreciate that," she said without thinking, immediately regretting mentioning anything about her body but especially that part.

Brady laughed but it didn't feel like he was laughing at her. "You'll have to come back in the winter so I can take you. You'd love it."

Butterflies bounced around in her stomach like they were on their own ATV. The way he said it felt different from an invitation to come back to the inn for a vacation. It felt much more personal, like...a date. She shouldn't overthink it. He was an activities director. His job was to get people to sign up for these kinds of things. Reading into his comment as though she was somehow special was dangerous. Brett had made it clear she was not special. It had been so easy to fall right out of love with her. Maybe he had never really been in love with her in the first place.

"Are you ready for some music?" Brady asked over the radio.

Anything would be a welcome distraction from Alexa's spiraling negative thoughts. "Bring it on."

Would he be an old soul who loved '70s rock? Would he be cringey and into whatever was trendy on pop radio? His playlist was going to give away something about Brady that she didn't know yet. The anticipation was almost too much.

Techno dance music blared through the speaker in her helmet. Not at all what she was expecting and a complete letdown. This was the kind of music he was into? It was terrible. She was just about to lower the volume when the music cut out.

"Kidding, kidding," Brady reassured her. "That was not my playlist."

Relieved laughter bubbled out of her. Alexa loved his sense of humor. She figured she'd tease him right back. "Wait, that was my favorite song! That's what they play in all the nightclubs in Manhattan."

"I will be forced to unpair us if that's true."

She definitely did not want him to do that. "Fine, I'm also kidding. I mean, it's possible they play that stuff in the clubs, but I have never been inside a New York nightclub, so I can't say for sure."

"Not a nightclubber. Good to know." He paused as they went over some rough terrain.

Once they were back on a smoother straight-away, he came back on the radio. "Okay, here is my real playlist."

A song came on that had a folk-pop sound, reminiscent of Paul Simon but fresh at the same time. The artist sang about Vermont and she fell in love with it a little more. Brady had a thing for New England–inspired music. Why was that so perfectly him?

His playlist was a combination of folk-pop, country, and rock. Alexa enjoyed each new song more than the last. Was it possible for someone's music choices to make them even more attractive than they already were?

Brady led the group off the trail and the sign Alexa passed read Jericho Warming Hut Ahead. Seeing that it was solidly in the seventies today, they certainly didn't need to take a break inside a warming hut.

The music stopped and the sound of Brady's voice filled her helmet. "First stop. Over and out for now."

Alexa pulled her ATV next to his and took off her helmet. She was grinning from ear to ear. "You have really good taste in music."

His eyebrows shot up. "Really? You liked it?"

"I'm going to need a copy of that playlist when we get back to the inn."

He nodded as the rest of the group pulled up

and parked. Richard complained that his pants had gotten muddy when they went through one of the puddles on the trail. Alexa knew that meant he had recklessly driven through it too fast. It was no one's fault but his.

"This is the warming hut," Brady explained. "In the winter, it's a great place to stop and… well, warm up. Inside, they keep a huge fireplace going and snowmobilers will stop and get some feeling back in their frozen fingers."

"Is there a restroom inside the hut?" Ivan asked.

Brady shook his head. "There are bathrooms on the other side of the main building if anyone needs to take a human moment. Otherwise, this is a good place to pull out your phones and snap a few pictures of this gorgeous valley." He spun around and raised his arms outward.

Alexa stepped forward and took in the sweeping view of the valley down below. It was a beautiful myriad of greens. The bright blue sky above was peppered with clouds that resembled wisps of smoke. A gentle haze softened the rocky outline of the mountains across the valley. The mountainside was covered in trees, but from this distance they looked black against the backdrop.

"You should see it in the fall when all the leaves turn color. It looks like a kaleidoscope of reds, oranges, and yellows from one side of the valley to the other."

Alexa took her phone out of her pocket. "So you're telling me I need to come back in the winter *and* the fall?"

"I mean, I'm not sure why you would want to leave, but if you have to, then yes."

This was only the fourth day of her vacation and she was beginning to wonder if she actually did want to leave. As she lifted her phone to take a photo, reality settled back in. Her screen was covered in text messages and a couple of missed-call notifications. It was Monday morning and there were probably a million emails waiting for her as well.

"Everything all right?" Brady asked as she stood there staring at her phone intently.

"Yeah, just work." She read through some of the texts. Neil had some questions, Jordan wanted her to look at the emails he had forwarded her, and there were a myriad of other requests from people who'd certainly gotten her automatic out-of-the-office reply to their emails.

She clicked out of messages and before she could hit the phone button, Brady took the phone out of her hand. "You, my dear, are on vacation. Work does not exist here in Jericho National Park. Smile for a picture so you can look back and remember how it felt to be free of responsibilities for just a little bit."

He held up the phone and flipped the camera

so it was front-facing. He put his arm around her shoulders. "Smile," he said, giving her a squeeze that sent a tingle down her spine. As soon as her lips curled upward, he took the selfie with the view of the valley behind them.

He handed her the phone back. "You all have ten minutes and then we're back on the trail. Use them wisely!" he announced to the group, all the while looking right at Alexa.

The phone calls could wait. The text messages could wait. She unlocked her phone and clicked on the photo app, so she could see the picture he took. His smile was dazzling. Hers was a bit strained, but at least she was smiling. It was a cute picture. She couldn't stop staring at it. The way they looked like a couple. The memory of how it felt to have his arm around her.

She was kidding herself. She knew better than to get caught up in some fantasy. The last year had taught her that. There was nothing wrong with enjoying Brady's company as long as she accepted that when her time in Apple Hollow was up, she would never see him again. Except on her phone in this picture. She clicked out of it and slid her phone back in her pocket.

"Do you think we'll see some wildlife?" Sofia, one of the women in their group, had Brady's attention for the moment.

"It's possible we could see some white-tailed

deer. Maybe we'll spot some black bears from a distance when we're up a little higher. They like to visit the streams."

"What about moose?" Richard asked. "I'm not leaving until I see a moose."

Alexa did not share that particular desire. She didn't want to see any more moose on this trip. One was enough.

Brady popped Richard's bubble. "I guess we'll be leaving without you, then. The moose tend to stay hidden in the cover of the woods. I don't think you're going to get any face time with a moose."

That was a relief. Alexa took one more look out over the valley. So much nature in one place. It had never bothered her to live in a concrete jungle before. She loved Central Park, but that was nothing compared to this. New Hampshire had more trees than people. That was not something New York City could boast.

Back on the trail, she listened to more of Brady's playlist. He would break in to tell her to look at something or give her some helpful suggestions on how to get through a particularly rough patch. There were several sections of the trail that were covered in half-buried boulders. She had to take her time and carefully navigate her way through them.

The second stop was an up-close view of enormous wind turbines. There were five of them and they looked almost alien on top of the mountain.

"When they brought these things into town, they had to shut down roads because they were so huge. One turbine came in on a dozen semi-trucks. Each blade got their own truck and escort."

Alexa took some more pictures, wanting to remember everything about this place. As they continued on, they drove around Jericho Lake. They passed by an RV park and campground. Summer travelers from all over the country came every year, according to Brady. He had friends who loved kayaking out here, but he preferred Lake Champney. They stopped for some pictures and Brady showed them where they could get the perfect shot of the mountains reflecting off the water.

Her favorite part of the ride was crossing an old railroad bridge to get to the waterfall at stop number four. She parked her ATV and took off her helmet. Taking a seat at one of the two picnic tables that sat alongside the road, she let herself relax and appreciate the view.

Brady slid into the seat next to her. "Having fun?"

"I had no idea what to expect, but this is so much better than I think I could have imagined.

I never realized all this was up here. I mean, I knew New Hampshire existed, but I had no idea how beautiful it was."

"I'm glad you took the opportunity to come and see it for yourself. I mean it when I say I hope you come back and visit us during other times of the year. I can't imagine living anywhere but here, and I love it when I convince someone else that it's as amazing as I think it is."

Alexa folded her hands together on the table. "A man of adventure like yourself doesn't have dreams of traveling the world to see what else it has to offer?"

Brady shrugged. "I am not against traveling, but this is home. I always come home."

Alexa loved the idea of home being a place she wanted to be. The city had its charm. She loved a good Broadway show or an even better off-Broadway gem. Her favorite bodega always had everything she needed. There were a million places to get a good meal. Still, her condo hadn't been a home for a while. Even before the divorce, she'd never raced home, and she couldn't put her finger on why. Hadn't she been in love with Brett from the moment they met? She'd thought they would be together forever. If she had really felt that way, then why didn't she want to be at home with him? He'd left her, but had she left him first? Brett had argued that once when they were fighting over who was going to move out.

You barely live here, Alexa. You sleep here. That's it, he had said.

"Where did you go?" Brady said, bringing her back to the present. "I think I lost you for a minute."

Her gaze lifted and she stared into the warmth of his brown eyes. He had a little scar above his right eyebrow. She wanted to know where he got it. There was sure to be some wild story that went along with it.

"Alexa." He placed a hand over both of hers. "What's going on in that pretty head of yours?"

"I hate that I only have a week left in my vacation. I don't think it's enough time."

His forehead scrunched up in confusion. "Enough time for what?"

To get to know everything about you. She stopped herself from saying it out loud, but that was how she felt. This was so different from the infatuation she had felt when she had met Brett back in college. Brady was not Brett. He was nothing like Brett.

"To forget why I left New York in the first place."

He took one of her hands in each of his. "We weren't built to forget. No matter how appealing forgetting sounds. We learn to move forward in spite of the things that make us feel bad. I'm sorry there's something you wish you could forget. I want you to remember that right here, right now, you're safe, you're in control, and you're doing just fine."

The tears came without warning. That was exactly what she needed to hear. It took all her self-control not to lean in and kiss him until she, at least for a moment, could forget her own name. Instead, she pulled out of his grasp and wiped her tears away.

"I think I need one of those human moments. Is there a restroom at this stop?"

Brady pressed his lips together in a slight grimace. "There is one, but it's a little ways down one of the hiking trails. I can take you, if you want."

He stood up, offered his hand to help her up, and didn't let go. Alexa needed something to break this spell he had put her under. There had to be some flaw, some chink in his white-knight armor. Before her time here was over, she would uncover it.

Tree roots crisscrossed the hiking path, and Brady carefully guided her over them. Some hikers with walking sticks passed them from the other direction as the wind rustled the leaves on the tree branches overhead. Alexa tried to focus on anything other than that feel of her hand in his as he led her to the restrooms.

Finally, there was a clearing and the outhouse facility. "I'll meet you back out here," Brady said, letting go.

Alexa took care of business and used her phone's camera to check her face to make sure there was no sign she had been crying. There was limited service out on the trails, but somehow those little service bars popped up and her phone rang with a call from Neil.

It had to be important if he was calling her on vacation. She had to answer it.

"Neil?"

"Oh, Alexa! I didn't expect you to pick up. I was j—" He cut out and Alexa moved around, hoping to find that sweet spot again.

"Neil, you're breaking up. Can you hear me?"

"I sa— He wa— But if y—"

Alexa kept searching for better reception. "You're still breaking up."

There was no sound coming from the other end anymore. She pulled her phone from her ear and checked to see if there were any bars. The call dropped as the no-service symbol appeared.

"Darn it!" Alexa held the phone out in front of her and waved it around high and low, hoping to get that signal back.

Twigs and leaves crunched and a familiar-sounding huff caught her attention. Standing in front of her was a moose about the same size as the one that had made her crash her rental car.

Frozen in place, Alexa's heart and lungs were the only parts of her body moving at full speed. Would it chase her if she ran away? Would it charge her if she stood still? What were the rules when facing down a moose?

"Stay calm," Brady said behind her. Thank goodness he was there. The moose tossed his head and stomped his foot. "It's okay, big guy. We're not here to bother you. Back away slowly, Alexa."

She did as he said and shuffled backward. The moose grunted. "Slowly, and maintain eye contact with him," he directed her. "It's all good, big man. We are going to leave you alone. We mean you no harm. No reason to get upset."

"Is he upset?" Alexa squeaked.

"He's a little agitated."

Alexa swallowed hard. The flight, fight, or freeze instinct that had been stuck on freeze was now strongly urging her to flee, but Brady kept reminding her to back up slowly. She felt his arms wrap around her as her back pressed against his front.

"I've got you," Brady assured her. "You're safe."

She knew it was true. Being in his embrace made her feel protected. If anyone was going to get her out of there unharmed, it was Brady.

Together they moved as one, backing farther and farther away from the moose, who stayed where he was but never broke eye contact. As they sidestepped to put the outhouse between them and the moose, Alexa could have sworn that the animal winked at her before it disappeared from view.

CHAPTER SIX

"And you didn't even get a picture?" Kayden asked Brady.

"It seemed safer to get out of there without pausing for photographs. I think we need to remember not all wildlife wants to end up on every human's social-media pages."

Kayden shook his head. "Missed opportunity, boss. When is that lady ever going to get that close to a moose again?"

The moose encounter was a hot topic back at the inn. Richard had been very unhappy about the fact that Alexa got to see a moose but it was gone by the time he went behind the outhouse to look for it. He'd had no qualms about questioning if they had even seen one when they got on the bus. Brady decided that meant it was all he was going to talk about. He had grabbed Kayden to help him set up the firepits on the lawn for the wildly popular Bonfires and S'mores night event later that evening.

"Hopefully never." Alexa's voice startled both of them.

Brady whirled around. "Hey."

"Hi." She had changed out of her trail outfit and into a flowy sundress. Her hair was down with the front pinned back so he could get a good look at her sun-kissed face. She had gotten a little pink after paddleboarding the other day. Her sunglasses were on, blocking a clear view of those eyes he was beginning to see when he closed his own at night.

"I think it's cool that you saw a moose. They don't usually let you get that close," Kayden said.

"Well, I've had two get up close and personal. I think that's enough for one trip."

"Two?" Brady wasn't aware she had already had a moose encounter.

"On my way here, there was one on the road. It caused me to drive into a tree and wreck my rental car. If you hadn't shown up, who knows what that one would have done to me today. I think they have it out for me. Not fans of New Yorkers maybe."

She made Brady and Kayden laugh. "I don't know if that's it." Brady narrowed an eye as he attempted to think of something clever to say. "Maybe they really like you and don't know what to say when you're close, so they just stand there awkwardly. You could be misreading the signs."

Alexa's face scrunched up. "I *know* that's not it. Although, I swear that moose winked at me. I think he enjoyed messing with me."

"Animals are smarter than you think," Kayden said, setting down one of the metal firepits. "We have squirrels that taunt our dog. They climb the tree behind our house and make noises at him until he loses his mind and my mom has to bring him in so the neighbors don't complain about the barking. It's like they know the poor guy can't climb trees."

Alexa's eyes flickered to Brady and her lips twitched with a suppressed smile. "Well, I just wanted to thank you again for rescuing me today, and for everything. Besides being possibly teased by a moose, I had a lot of fun."

Brady tipped his head slightly. "You're very welcome. I'm glad you enjoyed it. Are you coming to the Bonfires and S'mores event later? We have a no-moose policy—you should be safe."

She couldn't hold back her smile any longer. "I don't know if I can stay up that late. I'm exhausted from the day's activity."

A wave of disappointment swept over Brady and he hoped it didn't show on his face. "I bet there are workdays you are way more tired and still stay up past your bedtime to meet some deadline."

"That's a very valid point," she said. "I'll see what I can do. Maybe I'll find my second wind." She took a step back. "I'll let you two get back to your work. I just wanted you to know that I appreciate you. I mean, you know, appreciate your excellent service. As an activities director." Her blush not only flamed across her cheeks, but also flared over her chest and up her neck.

"Thank you. It's always good to hear you've done your job well."

Alexa nodded and nearly tripped over her own two feet as she attempted to retreat. She glanced nervously over her shoulder before making a mad dash back up the lawn toward the inn.

"She's funny. I like her," Kayden said, grabbing another firepit.

"I like her, too," Brady said, watching her make her escape. He really did love the way she looked when flustered.

"I think she might like you, if we're being honest here," Kayden said.

Brady snapped out of his Alexa-induced haze. "Says the teenager who has had how many girlfriends in his lifetime?"

Kayden chuckled. "Just because I haven't had a ton of girlfriends doesn't mean I can't tell when a girl likes someone."

"First of all, that's a woman, not a girl. Second, she's a guest. She was simply letting me know that we are making her stay enjoyable. That's what guests do. Third, I am a professional. I am not looking for someone to like me."

The kid wore an amused grin. "Okay, whatever you say."

Brady put another firepit on the lawn. Great, even Kayden was calling him out. He had made a promise to his dad, but Alexa wasn't helping him keep it. He liked being around her. It made him happy to get a smile or a giggle out of her. The way she thought about the world was interesting, and there were so many questions he had because he wanted to know everything about her.

"Brady Robert Seasons." Nora's expression was unreadable as she trudged down the lawn, but the use of his middle name was concerning. Brady checked his watch. Her shift had just ended.

Kayden, looking like a scared puppy, put some space between him and Brady. No one messed with Nora. What could he have done to make her so mad? As she got closer, he could tell she was actually smiling.

He was so confused. Was she mad at him or pleased? "What did I do?"

She stopped in front of him. "Thank you for

whatever you did to put Ms. Fox and Mr. Leroy together today. I may have accidentally walked by when she was on the phone with her friend while she was relaxing in the sunroom. I may have overheard her talking about how *he* is so funny and she hasn't felt like this in such a long time. I told you I was right."

Brady's eyebrows pinched together. Alexa was talking to someone about Richard? Unlikely. Unless she was sharing that she hadn't been this annoyed by someone in a long time, there was no way she was talking about him.

"She said Richard Leroy was so funny?"

"Well, no. She said 'he.'"

"So you just assumed that she was talking about him?"

"Who else would it be? The other two guys are here with their significant others. Unless..." Her eyes bulged. "Do we have a scandal on our hands? Did you notice anything?"

Kayden snorted. Brady shot him a warning look before turning to his sister. The last thing he wanted was for Nora to think badly of Alexa. "I did not notice anything unsavory going on. She really didn't talk to anyone except maybe the other ladies. But I am not paying attention to everything going on every minute. Maybe your matchmaking worked."

"Of course it did. I'm good at this. I told you!"

She was so pleased with herself, Brady didn't have the heart to tell her the truth. The truth could very likely be that Alexa had been talking about Brady. The thought made him want to do a celebratory touchdown dance. He couldn't do that, though. She was a guest and he had made his dad a promise. It was better that Nora believed the lie that Alexa and Richard were having a wonderful time together.

"Are you staying for the bonfire tonight?" he asked her, changing the subject.

"Can't. Blair and I are going to watch Wade play softball. His team is undefeated and they play the other team in their league that's undefeated, so tonight is a big night." Blair was Nora's best friend and Wade was Blair's brother. He was also the head of maintenance at the inn.

"Wish him luck for me."

"I will," she promised as she hurried off.

"Boy, I wonder who Ms. Fox could have been talking about if it wasn't Mr. Leroy," Kayden mused aloud, daring to tease his boss.

Brady tipped his chin in the direction of the remaining firepits. "Why don't you finish this up instead of worrying about how guests feel about each other? I'm going to check to see if my mom needs any help."

He really needed to be more careful about how he talked to Alexa. Especially around the other people who worked at the inn. If word got back to his dad, or, heaven forbid, Quinn, Brady wouldn't hear the end of it.

Why did it make him happy to think it was him? There really wasn't anyone she spent more time with than Brady. He also wasn't imagining the way she looked at him or the way she trembled a bit when he touched her. Even Kayden noticed how nervous she was talking to him. It was satisfying that she might be feeling the same way he was.

Did any of that matter? Was she going to move to Apple Hollow? Was he going to move to New York? Both questions could only be answered with resounding no's. Not to mention, hadn't he decided that relationships were off the table for him after what Sabrina had done to him? Funny, he hadn't thought about Sabrina once since spending time with Alexa.

Brady scrubbed his face with both hands. He was in trouble if he didn't get his head on straight. He wasn't sure what was happening to him, but he needed to get it under control.

He found his mom, Laura, in the kitchen, preparing desserts for the dinner guests who would be flooding the restaurant soon. His mom always seemed frozen in time. It was only in the last couple of years that Brady had started to notice that she had a few more lines around her eyes and a little more gray showing along her hairline. She always wore her long brown hair in a bun. She often joked that she should have been born back when the first settlers arrived in Apple Hollow. She loved to wear prairie dresses and was never without her white apron in the kitchen. It was perfect that she shared the same name with the little girl from *Little House on the Prairie*.

"Can I do anything to help with the s'mores party?" he asked, snatching a brownie from the platter she was putting together.

She bumped him with her hip. "Get out of there, Brady. I know you're going to eat a thousand marshmallows tonight. That's more than enough sugar for you."

It was true. Brady loved toasted marshmallows. He had the biggest sweet tooth of all the Seasons kids. Some might say he was a sugar addict. There was a time when he was young when they had a doctor suggest that they restrict his sugar intake to help with his attention deficit and hyperactivity. It was the worst two weeks of his life and didn't make him any less energetic, but it did make him crabby. His mom decided a happy, hyper kid was better than an irritable one, and sugar was allowed again in moderation.

"I really did come in here to help."

Her lips thinned and her skepticism was evident in the furrow of her brow. "We have it all under control. Why don't you go clean up? You've been working hard all day and deserve a nice shower."

That was her nice way of saying he stunk. He lifted his arm and gave himself a sniff. She wasn't wrong. Good thing she mentioned it. The last thing he wanted was to talk to Alexa tonight smelling ripe.

"What time is the family eating tonight?" Since they all lived on the property, they tended to eat meals together after their mom took care of things at the inn's restaurant.

"Your dad said he's grilling burgers tonight. I would say you have an hour before we sit down."

He gave her a kiss on the cheek and snagged one more brownie before he dashed out of there. The Seasonses had a house on the far west side of the property. It had a clear view of the lake and was surrounded by some of the tallest sugar maples, giving them a little sense of privacy.

Brady cleaned up and found his dad on the back deck, grilling some burgers just like his mom had said. The old man wasn't much of a cook. He left that to their mom most of the time, but he loved firing up the grill in the summer.

"Can I do anything?" Brady asked, cracking open the can of soda he had snatched from the fridge on his way out.

"Can you grab the hamburger buns off the

kitchen counter? Your brother likes his bun toasted."

Brady noticed Quinn wasn't anywhere to be seen. "Is he actually going to join us for dinner and not work overtime tonight?"

"We're all going to work overtime tonight. It's s'mores night."

He knew what Brady meant. Quinn was always working. Brady could swear there were nights his brother didn't even come back to the house to sleep. He had a theory that Quinn slept in an unoccupied room at the inn so he was always on hand to take care of emergencies. His brother was dedicated to being the one whom their dad trusted to leave in charge when the old man finally decided to retire. Brady wondered if that was ever going to happen, though. He couldn't imagine the Seasons Inn without Gavin Seasons. It was quite possible that his dad would work until his time here on earth came to an end.

He grabbed the hamburger buns just as Quinn arrived home. "Look who decided to take a dinner break."

"I don't have a ton of time. I need to make sure Ivy has everything she needs for the event tonight."

"Kayden and I set up all the firepits. Mom said she has everything under control with the s'mores. You don't have anything to worry about."

"There's always a million things to worry about. But you wouldn't know about that, would you? You never worry about anything."

His cutting remark took Brady aback. "What's that supposed to mean?"

Quinn shook his head. "You just don't have any idea what it takes to run this business. You get to play all day while I'm putting out a million fires."

It wasn't unusual for Quinn to act superior, but for him to insinuate that Brady didn't know what it took to run the hotel was a blow to his ego. "I'm sorry that I chose to take on the responsibility of entertaining the guests. I know it may seem like all I do is have fun, but I do a lot to make sure things go off without any major issues. You might be handling things inside the inn, but I am the one coordinating the excursions and managing the well-being of everyone I take off the property. There are plenty of business issues that I handle that never cross your desk, by the way."

"Right, because you don't like to send emails or attend the director meetings so we can all be on the same page. You like flying by the seat of your pants." Quinn pushed past his brother and opened the sliding glass doors to join their dad on the deck.

Brady felt like he was missing some context

to that argument. He wasn't aware that he hadn't been living up to some expectations Quinn had of him. Quinn was the oldest of the siblings. He had also always been the most intense. He was the overachiever and the one who felt like he had to be perfect at everything.

That was a lot to live up to, especially for Brady, who'd been diagnosed with ADHD when he was nine. ADHD impacted everything he did academically. While Quinn had been valedictorian of his graduating class, Brady had paid Kelsey Jessop twenty bucks a pop to write his essays so he could pass English with a D-plus every year.

Brady had grown up with two overachieving brothers. Brady was three years older than Theo and three years younger than Quinn. Theo wasn't the brainiac Quinn was, but was a superstar on the ice. He currently played hockey professionally for the Boston Icemen. He didn't want anything to do with the inn, but he was living the dream and no one was about to deny him a chance to do that. It did leave Brady to be Quinn's punching bag, however.

"Food will be ready in a couple minutes," his dad said as Brady followed his brother outside.

He handed his dad the package of buns. "Good, because it seems Quinn is a little hangry."

"I'm not hangry. I'm frustrated because I

spent half my day with Wade trying to figure out what he can do about the outdated electrical system in the north wing that's apparently the reason the breakers keep tripping multiple times a day in the rooms on the second floor. Unfortunately, what we learned was that he is in no way qualified to do anything about it, so I spent the other half calling electricians, hoping to find someone to come out and not charge us an arm and a leg because an enormous bill to an outside contractor is the last thing we need right now."

"There's got to be something Wade can do to get us through the summer. We'll be able to spend a little extra this fall on a real fix," their dad said. He was famous for putting Band-Aids on things until he could afford to do things the right way. Poor Wade was always being asked to find makeshift solutions to save the day temporarily.

Quinn shook his head. "He's over his head on this one. He doesn't have enough experience with electrical stuff. Plus, there's only so much he can do with stuff that's so outdated."

"I've been telling you guys that we have to start moving into the new century one of these days," Brady chimed in. "We don't have enough outlets in the rooms and these days families need to charge multiple devices at night. I've seen these cool new outlets where they have the

USB charger integrated into them, so people can charge four devices at one outlet."

"Have you looked into what that would entail? Would we have to rewire the whole inn? Do you have any idea how much money it would cost to redo all the outlets?" Quinn asked, his arms folded over his chest.

"I haven't talked to an electrician if that's what you mean. I'm just acknowledging there is an issue and an improvement we could make that would make a real difference for our guests."

"But that costs money, Brady. I'd love to see you put together a proposal to make changes instead of just spouting off things you think are cool."

"Hey, don't attack your brother for having ideas." His dad was mopping the sweat off his forehead with a paper towel.

"He has these ideas but no plan. He expects me to figure out all the rest of it. I don't have time to investigate my ideas and his," Quinn complained.

"I can come up with a plan. I will come up with a plan. Giving people more outlets was only one part of my plan. I have a lot of ideas, and I will happily write up some little proposal for you if that'll make you stop being such a jerk."

"Okay, that's enough, you two. If your mother comes home and hears you talking to each other like this, she'll have a fit. The Seasons Inn belongs to all of us. We are all invested in making it the best it can be. We all are responsible for its success or failure. I love that you're both passionate about doing your part. At the same time, we are a family, and we treat each other with respect and love. I don't want any more of this name-calling or constant criticism. We're all on the same team."

The sliding glass door opened and their mom came out to join them. Having been properly scolded, both Brady and Quinn were quiet. Their mom knew that meant there had been trouble.

"What did I miss?" she asked, closing the door behind her.

"Nothing. You're right on time for dinner. Let's eat. The boys are both a bit hangry."

Brady hadn't been angry until Quinn decided to spread his misery around. One thing was for sure, he was going to write a darned proposal. He was going to show his family he wasn't playing around.

CHAPTER SEVEN

ALEXA SHOULDN'T HAVE been looking for him, but she couldn't keep herself from scanning the crowd for Brady. He had said he would be here. He had asked her to come. A personal invitation was all she had needed to find her second wind.

"Can I offer you a marshmallow-roasting stick?" one of the young women working the event asked as Alexa walked by.

The only way not to look like some kind of stalker was to participate in the night's activity. "Thanks."

"You can get your marshmallows and the rest of your fixings at the table over there." The girl pointed. "Then, feel free to use any of the firepits to heat things up."

Alexa smiled and made it over to the sweets. If he was here, he would find her. Unless he was busy with other guests. He could have very easily invited many of the guests to this event.

She jabbed a huge marshmallow onto the end of her stick. It was embarrassing that she had told Melody she was having the best time mainly because of a certain someone who was paying her a bit of extra attention.

Once more, Alexa scanned the lawn, which was dotted with about a dozen lit firepits. Families and couples huddled around them, the fires casting an orange glow across their faces.

"Alexa!" Sofia called from her circle of friends. "Come roast your marshmallow with us."

The whole gang was around the bonfire. Sofia and Ivan were married and Margo and Leo were engaged. The men were cousins, including Richard, who was not married, engaged, or otherwise spoken for. Another couple Alexa had seen around but hadn't met was also standing by the same firepit.

"Alexa is the one who almost got attacked by a moose today," Sofia said to the new people.

The woman put her hand over her heart. "Oh, my gosh! Was that the scariest thing you have ever experienced?"

"I don't know that he was planning to attack me. He was really just standing there in the woods. I was pretty freaked out, though."

"Alexa, this is Maeve and her husband, Nathan," Sofia said, introducing them. Maeve looked like she was a former college cheerleader, and Nathan probably played some college sport back in the day. Maeve was petite and probably wore a size zero. Nathan was tall with the beginnings of a dad bod. They seemed around Alexa's age. "They were going to sign up for the ATV excursion and changed their minds last minute."

"We're kicking ourselves now that we heard it was filled with so much adventure," Maeve said. "I don't know what I would have done if that happened to me."

"Yeah, right," her husband said with a laugh. "You probably would have taken a selfie and given him a nickname."

She playfully elbowed him in the ribs. "I would not!"

He continued to tease her. "Maeve is never without her phone. It's like it's attached to her hand."

"Well, one of us has to preserve the memories. You never take a picture of anything. Please tell me you got a picture," Maeve said, turning her attention back to Alexa.

"She didn't. She stood in front of one of the most majestic creatures in this part of the world and didn't even take one photo," Richard complained. It was a real sticking point for him for some reason. He had been the one who'd wanted to see a moose more than anything. She understood being a little jealous, but Richard acted like she had run into the moose on purpose just to one-up him.

"I was holding my phone and never even thought to take a picture of it. If it wasn't for Brady, I would probably still be standing there, frozen like a statue."

"Oh, Brady, the activities guy?" Maeve yanked her stick out of the fire, her marshmallow aflame. She blew on it until it was nothing but a blackened blob. "He's hotter than this marshmallow. If I wasn't married, I would be signed up to go on every activity run by that guy."

Nathan held out his hands in disbelief. "I'm standing right here, babe."

"Oh, you know I'm kidding." She turned to Alexa and mouthed, *I'm not kidding*, then dissolved into giggles.

"It sure seems like everyone is having a good time over here." Brady appeared out of nowhere and was talking to everyone but looking right at Alexa.

"Speak of the devil," Ivan said. "We were just talking about how you saved Alexa from the killer moose today."

It was funny how they kept trying to amp up the story. Alexa pressed her lips together and exchanged a look with Brady.

He placed a hand on his forehead. "Can you imagine what kind of reviews we'd get on the internet if I let the guests get attacked by moose on an inn-sponsored activity?"

"That would not be good for business," Nathan agreed.

"Oh, come on, it would have made this place go viral. 'Woman attacked by a moose' would be all over the news," Richard said, waving his stick around.

"Sorry my coming out of the experience unscathed isn't very exciting. I am, however, not a big believer in all press is good press. I think Brady was wise to get me out of there and avoid the headlines."

"Listen, I'm in marketing. There is no such thing as bad press. If your name is out there, people are talking about you. If people are talking about you, you get brand awareness. Brand awareness leads to sales."

"Are you serious?" Alexa laughed.

"This is probably over your head. Brand awareness is how familiar people are with—"

"I am well aware of what brand awareness is." She did not need Richard to mansplain anything about marketing to her.

The man had the nerve to laugh. "Oh, I'm sorry, did you graduate from Boston College with a business degree?"

She knew better than to engage with someone who was clearly so full of himself that it wasn't going to matter what she said, but she couldn't resist. "I actually have a business degree from NYU. I double majored in accounting and finance. I got my master's in accountancy, passed the CPA, and got my first job at one of the big four accounting firms. I worked out of their Manhattan office for a few years, got promoted to manager early. Then, I went and got my MBA from Columbia, left my job at the accounting firm, and currently do work as a consultant for Roger Gatton. But, please, tell me more about what you know about brand awareness."

The entire group went silent. The only sounds coming from their bonfire area were the crackling logs on the fire.

"I think I'm going to side with Ms. Fox on this one. She seems to be the most qualified," Brady said, breaking the silence. "Which reminds me... Can I bother you for a second?" He looked at Alexa expectantly.

"Sure." She wished everyone a good night, meaning it for everyone but Richard. She hoped his s'more gave him indigestion.

"I think I might need to call 911," Brady said as he led her away from the s'mores event and closer to the pool.

"Why? What's wrong?" Alexa scanned the area in front of them for some kind of emergency.

He stopped and pivoted to face her. "I think you might have murdered that man back there.

I mean, I am fairly certain that his ego is completely destroyed."

Alexa grimaced. "That was mean, wasn't it? I shouldn't be such a braggart." That was another thing Brett had had an issue with when they were married. He hated anytime she talked about Columbia because it was as if she was trying to prove she was better than him.

Brady's brow furrowed. "What are you talking about? That was awesome! He was the one trying to act like a know-it-all. You served him a big ol' hunk of humble pie. He needed it."

He seemed so enthusiastic about it, she wasn't going to argue. "I hate when people assume what I know or don't know. It's always been an ick for me."

"Same. Of course, I probably don't know more than I know, but it's nice to be given the benefit of the doubt most times."

"I get that." She was still holding her roasting stick with the marshmallow perched at the tip. Now that she wasn't by the fire, it seemed weird for her to be standing there with it. "Was there something you wanted to talk to me about?"

"Yes. I was wondering if I could pick your brain. All those things you said to Richard made me realize that you are not only funny, beautiful, and charming, but you are also supersmart when it comes to business."

Alexa's heart stuttered in her chest. Did he just say she was funny, beautiful, and charming? She hadn't felt those things in a while. It took a moment for her to realize that he was waiting for her to say something.

"You want to do what?"

"Pick your brain. See, I can come up with lots of ideas. I think that my ideas could really help the inn. The problem is that I am not much of anything past the idea man. I need some help figuring out how to sell my idea to my dad and brother—mostly my dad, because he always has the final say."

"You want me to help you figure out a business plan?"

Brady pointed his finger at her. "Yes, that. A business plan. I need to come up with a business plan. Is that similar to what you do? I know you're on vacation. I don't want to interfere with your relaxing and not thinking about business plans. I would totally understand if you told me to go jump—"

"Yes. I would absolutely like to help you put together a business plan."

His brown eyes widened, along with his smile. "Yes? You'll help me?"

"You saved me from a killer moose, according to Ivan. I think I owe you."

Without warning, he wrapped his arms around

her and hugged her tightly. "Thank you, thank you, thank you!"

Alexa could smell the soap on his skin. His body was warm and his arms were so strong. Maybe if she helped him write the best business plan of all time, he would be willing to give her another hug just like this one.

He loosened his hold and drew back slightly. "You are so very kind. I know it's asking a lot."

"I write business plans in my sleep, Brady. Don't sweat it."

There was a noise behind them and two kids came running out of some bushes, chasing each other and laughing. The interruption led to Brady taking a step back and letting her go. She missed being in his arms immediately.

"I work all day. I don't suppose you'd be willing to meet up tomorrow evening?"

"I think that would be perfect. I'm staying in the Garden Suite. There's plenty of space for us to sit and brainstorm. What time should I expect you?"

"Seven?" he offered.

"It's a date." Alexa wanted to suck those words back in as soon as they came out. Brady took it in stride but his face definitely reacted to the word *date*.

"I will see you then. We should get you back

to the bonfire." He started to walk in that direction but stopped. "Can I ask one other favor?"

She shrugged. "I don't see why not."

"Can we keep this between you and me? I would really appreciate it if no one else knew you were helping me, especially anyone related to me, anyone who works here. I'm not sure how my family would feel about me imposing on a guest to help improve business."

Alexa felt some of the joy escape from the happy bubble she had been standing in. He wanted to keep it a secret because any kind of relationship with her outside of being guest and activity director would be inappropriate. She had known that, but to hear him basically say it stung a little.

"Your secret is safe with me," she assured him.

He gave her a relieved smile. "Thanks. I'll see you tomorrow." He turned to go but stopped again. "What does my sister have planned for you tomorrow?"

"Tennis lesson in the morning."

His eyes narrowed. "Not with me."

"Another massage at the spa."

He frowned. "Also not with me."

"And I think there's something about visiting the markets in downtown Apple Hollow tomorrow afternoon."

His grin was back. "That's with me. I'm glad

I'm going to see you before I see you. You know, earlier than we just planned to meet. Earlier than seven." He struggled, fumbling to find his way to the right words. "I'll be the one escorting guests into town."

"I picked up on that."

"See?" He snapped his fingers and pointed at her. "You're smart. We've established that. We should go."

Alexa's cheeks hurt from smiling so hard. It was nice that she wasn't always the one unsure of what to say or how to act in these moments.

He led her back to the main lawn, where they got a new plate of chocolate and graham crackers. After plucking off the marshmallow that had most likely gone stale on her stick, he replaced it with a fresh one and got himself one as well. They didn't rejoin Sofia and the rest of her group. Brady took her to a bonfire they could have all to themselves.

"I feel like there are a lot of interesting things I don't know about you," he said, holding his marshmallow over the fire.

Alexa began roasting hers, too. His comment got her thinking. "Interesting" wasn't how she would describe herself. Driven. Competent at work. Those might be positive things someone could say about her. None of it was super interesting.

"I'm a workaholic. My ex would tell you it makes me very boring."

"I am also a workaholic and I'm *super* interesting, so I don't buy it. Let's play a game. I tell you something about me and you tell me that same thing about you. For example, I have two brothers and one sister. You have met my sister, Nora, and my older brother, Quinn. My younger brother, Theo, lives in Boston. None of them are married, so I have no brothers- or sisters-in-law. Now, you go."

"I have an older brother named Glenn, who lives in Philadelphia. He's married to Natalia, my sister-in-law. They have two kids, Maggie and Beckett."

"So you're an aunt. That's interesting."

"I don't see them very often. Maybe every other Christmas and maybe one other time during the year. I'm terrible at making time to go to Philly to visit. My sister-in-law loves to post about their family life on social media, so I guess I've kept up with what's going on electronically. It's something that I want to change, though. My brother was really there for me during my divorce. The last year has taught me that I need to put more time into the relationships that are important to me."

"I feel that way about my brother Theo. The rest of the family lives and works here. We take for granted that we get to see each other every day, but Theo barely comes home. It takes effort to keep long-distance relationships strong, and I'll be honest, he's not the only one to blame for not making it a priority."

Alexa's marshmallow was ready to make into a s'more. She started stacking the ingredients, using the top and the bottom to smash the marshmallow in the middle and slide it off the stick.

"I am a terrible cook, but this thing looks delicious," she said before taking a bite. A string of melted marshmallow clung to the s'more and her lip. She laughed as she tried to detach it without making too much of a mess.

Brady constructed his s'more, and once again found common ground. "I am also a terrible cook. But to be fair, I live and work here and can eat at the restaurant whenever I want. My mother is also an amazing pastry chef. If you've eaten any of the sweets the restaurant has to offer, you know what I'm talking about."

"Oh, those pastries in the morning…yum." Alexa was sure to gain ten pounds on this trip thanks to those things.

"Exactly. Why would I cook?"

They ate their s'mores and both made messes of themselves. He had chocolate smeared in the corner of his mouth and she had marshmallow all over her fingers. Brady ran over to the banquet table and snagged them a few wet wipes to clean up.

"I love movies but can't watch them in a movie theater because I cannot sit still for that long. I have to watch them at home, so I can move around the room."

Alexa quirked an eyebrow. "That is very interesting."

"I have hyperactivity issues. Teachers used to love me," he said, rolling his eyes. "One of the criteria for ADHD is acting as if driven by a motor. I was born with the engine of a Bugatti. It's got horsepower to spare."

"I had a friend in high school who had ADHD and we had AP Psych together. I still remember he did a presentation on ADHD and listed all these famous people who shared the same diagnosis. You're in really good company. Einstein was on that list. I'll never forget how shocked everyone was. People don't realize that there are advantages to being differently abled."

"I never thought of it that way, as an advantage. It's always seemed like something I had to overcome. I mean, it helps in my current job, but when I was in school, I wished I had Einstein's kind of ADHD. Okay, your turn."

"I'm not sure if I'm supposed to say something about a thing that I love that's got a weird twist or tell you about a quirk of mine."

"I'll take either."

Alexa pondered her life for a moment. Surely, there were some quirky things she could share. "Um, I love dogs, but I have never had a pet. Not even a goldfish growing up. My mom refused to let animals in the house. She said she knew that if we were allowed to have a pet, she would end up being the one who had to take care of it in the end. When I got old enough and moved out on my own, I was too busy to have one. But maybe I should just get a dog."

"It's important to think about the dog and its needs before you rush out and get one. You have to be really ready to take care of it. Your mom was also not wrong. We've had four dogs in my lifetime, and without a doubt, my mom fed them, walked them, made sure they had water, cleaned up after them, and took them to the vet more than the rest of us combined."

"My mother is rarely wrong. Even when she is, she could convince us that she was not." She sighed before continuing. "I think you convinced me not to get a dog after all. I know I could do right by a dog, but maybe not at this time in my life."

"Cats, on the other hand, are very self-sufficient. If you want to try pet ownership at some point, a cat might be more manageable."

Alexa shook her head. "I am not a cat person. My eyes feel itchy just talking about them."

"No cats. All right." He snapped his fingers. "I got it. Moose seem to like you. Maybe you could move up here and start a moose sanctuary."

She frowned before breaking into giggles. "No thank you. I do *not* think moose like me. They make me crash my car. They stare me down in the woods and scare the bejesus out of me. I want nothing to do with them."

"You did look pretty terrified. Thank goodness I was there to save the day. Who knows what would have happened."

Fighting a smile, she played along. "Who knows? I could still be trying to win that staring contest. I don't like to lose. Have I mentioned that yet?"

His eyebrows rose and his eyes opened. "Me, either! That is a result of having two brothers who were better at everything I wanted to be good at. I can't stand losing."

"My competitive nature always gets the best of me. I'm sure I will either come back from those tennis lessons tomorrow the happiest winner or the sorest loser. Even if they don't have me actually compete against someone, I will be competing in my head, and if I'm not good enough to hold my own against Serena Williams, then I am a lost cause."

"Serena Williams? Maybe the greatest tennis player of all time? That Serena Williams?"

"That's the one."

"Tomorrow will be how many times you've held a tennis racket?"

"The first."

Brady nodded at her absurdity. "Of course. Right, why not set those expectations high?" His expression changed as his eyebrows tugged together. "How come you gave up so fast on the paddleboard, Miss Competitive? You went down once and stayed on your knees the rest of the time."

"Paddleboarding wasn't a competitive sport. That was a leisurely tour-guided paddle around the lake. Totally different."

"Ahhh. So if I had asked you all to race around the lake, you would have tried harder?"

"Um, *yes*," she said definitively. "I would have blown Donovan out of the water. He thought he was the fastest for sure."

"Teenage-boy confidence. It's a disease."

Once again, Alexa found herself laughing. She seemed to do that a lot when she was with Brady. It felt so good. If she didn't have a million things waiting for her back in New York, she would extend this vacation indefinitely. The sad truth was it was almost half over.

"Brady!" a woman in a Seasons Inn polo shirt

called from a few yards away. "Can you help me with something?"

He nodded and sighed. "Duty calls. It was really nice getting to know you better. And for the record, I think you are one of the most interesting people I have met in a long time."

Alexa felt a lightness inside that had been missing for some time now. "I appreciate that. I agree with your earlier claim—you *are* super interesting."

"What can I say? I'm also very humble," he said, making her laugh. "Good night, Alexa. I'll see you tomorrow after you crush it on the tennis courts and relax at the spa."

The tingling in her stomach was distracting, but she did not want this moment to end. "Good night, Brady."

Unfortunately, he had to go back to work, and she was once again alone. She hated being alone, but tonight she realized that being alone was better than being with someone who didn't find her interesting. She didn't need Brett to make her life complete. Maybe losing Brett would turn out to be a good thing, instead of the thing that made her feel like she was a failure.

CHAPTER EIGHT

By lunchtime on Tuesday, Brady had already taken two groups out in kayaks, helped Wade replace a section of the fencing around the pool, and stolen three cookies from the kitchen. He had checked in with Rory, the tennis pro they employed to give tennis lessons to guests. Without asking specifically about Alexa, he learned that Rory had one guest who showed some real promise for her first time. That had to be Alexa.

"If you are here to take another cookie, I will ban you from the kitchen permanently, Brady," his mother warned.

He held his hands up to prove he wasn't trying to get away with anything. "Can't a boy want to say hello to his mom?"

"Hello, sweetheart. Now, get out of here. Go make yourself a sandwich at home. Something with a little more sustenance than sugar."

"If you weren't so good at making things that have sugar in them, I wouldn't be so tempted to eat them. Plus, I'm bored of sandwiches."

She shook her head, not buying what he was selling. She might not want him to eat any more sweets, but she wouldn't deny him some lunch. "Armand will make you something if you don't want to go back to the house."

Armand was the head chef. For the last ten years, he had been feeding Brady at least once a day. Brady clapped his hands together. "What's the lunch special today?"

"I made clam chowder with bacon and scallions. You could have it with a side salad. It will make your mother happy if you put some vegetables in your body," Armand said as he sautéed something in a pan.

"Mmm, I do love your clam chowder. I guess a salad won't kill me."

"It's unfair that someone who eats as many calories as you do a day looks as fit as you do," Armand said enviously. He was a portly man. He enjoyed food—cooking it and eating it.

"If we all ran around this property as much as Brady did, we'd all be that slim and trim," his mom replied. "No one has that boy's energy."

No one argued that point. Brady got his lunch and went out into the dining room to find a quiet table to sit down and eat. His eyes were immediately drawn to Alexa, who was seated alone with a glass of lemonade in front of her as she perused the menu. Brady glanced around. No sign of his dad or Quinn. They usually ran home to eat if they took a lunch at all. The dining room felt as safe as any place.

He leaned down and quietly asked, "Mind if I join you for lunch?"

She was startled, although he had not meant for that to happen. She pressed the menu to her chest. "Hi."

She made him smile. "Hi. May I?" He nodded at the seat across from her.

"Is it okay if someone sees us together?"

"We're safe. I don't want to intrude, though, so feel free to tell me to go away if you want."

"No, please, sit. I'm not a fan of eating in restaurants by myself, but I came here alone to push myself out of my comfort zone. I'd love some company, though."

Brady sat down and set his soup and salad on the table. "Benefits of knowing everyone in the kitchen. I can run back there and get you something faster than any server, if you want me to."

"No, no. It's fine. You probably have time constraints. Eat. I'm sure my waitress will be back any second."

"How were your tennis lessons this morning?" he asked before taking a bite of his chowder.

Alexa's face lit up. "I think I did pretty good. I might not be Serena Williams, but I was better at it than I thought I would be."

"I think you may have found a new hobby to take back with you to New York. They have tennis courts there, don't they? Are they like on the rooftops of all those tall skyscrapers?"

She laughed at his silliness. "We have plenty of tennis courts in the city. We squeeze them in on the ground in between all the tall skyscrapers. Can you imagine what a hazard it would be to walk around Manhattan if tennis balls were falling out of the sky after every bad shot?"

"Good point. That's why I am not an architect. I wouldn't know where to put the tennis courts."

"Hey, Brady." Erin, one of the servers, appeared beside their table. She seemed genuinely confused as to why he was sitting with a guest.

"Good afternoon, Erin. I'm here to make sure that Ms. Fox gets quality service today. She was almost attacked by a moose yesterday and we decided that we needed to take extra special care of her the rest of her stay. I'm glad she got you. I know you're going to treat her right."

Erin's gaze shifted to Alexa. "Oh, you're the guest who saw the moose. I heard about that. We're all glad you weren't hurt. Those things are way bigger in person, aren't they?"

"Huge," Alexa said with a nod. "Can I get what he has? That looks delicious."

"Absolutely." Erin glanced at the food in front

of Brady. "Clam chowder and a side salad. I'll have that out for you in a jiffy."

The young server took off. Brady stabbed a cherry tomato with his fork. "This is delicious. Good call."

"Why is my moose sighting such a big deal around here? Don't you see moose all the time?"

"They are a bit more evasive than you think. They tend to come out around dawn and dusk, especially in the summer months. You might catch one getting a drink by a pond. People pay good money to have guides take them out looking for them, and oftentimes, they come up empty-handed."

"I had no idea that this would be my claim to fame. I feel bad I didn't get a picture now."

"If you want me to take you into the woods and see if we can find another one, I can," Brady offered, but she was quick to refuse.

"Nope, no way. No thank you. Like I said, two moose were enough."

"I think we have stuffed moose in the gift shop. You could take one of those home and tell everyone that was what they looked like."

"Perfect."

She was perfect. Brady couldn't stop staring into her eyes. Green eyes were so rare and hers were such an interesting shade. They reminded him of a lush green valley when the sun was directly overhead, when everything had a brightness about it.

"Here's your chowder and your salad," Erin said, setting the food in front of Alexa and pulling Brady out of his haze.

They ate lunch together, and Brady was surprised at how normal it felt. Spending time with Alexa put him at ease. His thoughts weren't racing, he wasn't antsy to move on to the next thing. He was content to be still if it meant getting to look at her, listen to her thoughts, be close enough to touch.

She dabbed her mouth with her napkin. "That was the best clam chowder I've ever had."

"I feel like we need to book your next stay here before you leave. This week is not enough time for me to give you the full experience. There are so many more things to do, to eat, to see. I want you to try it all."

Alexa set her napkin back in her lap and her gaze dropped as she smoothed it out. "I wish I could commit to something. My job—" She didn't seem to know how to finish that sentence, but Brady understood.

She had a life back in New York. She had a job and responsibilities. She had friends and family. Coming here to spend time with him did not make sense in the grand scheme of her life. He needed to stop letting his heart get carried away.

He also couldn't forget that she was still nursing a broken heart. Her divorce was probably a lot harder to get over than his breakup with Sabrina.

"No, I get it. We're trained to encourage repeat business, you know. It's been ingrained in me to push for another booking," he said in an attempt at saving face. "Gotta fill those rooms. Empty rooms mean an empty bank account."

Those green eyes lifted to meet his. "Right. I should have known that. Richard would be roasting me right now for not recognizing the sales strategy. You're very good at your job."

He was terrible. He had meant every word and his desire to have her come back had nothing to do with the inn, with sales, or anything other than wanting more time with her.

"Speaking of my job, I should probably get back to it." Brady stood and pushed in his chair. "Thank you for letting me crash your lunch. I'll see you when we load up the van to go to town."

She looked up at him and smiled in a way that seemed forced. "Can't wait."

Brady couldn't get out of the dining room fast enough. He tried to zip through the lobby to get to the parking lot to make sure the van was gassed and ready to go. Nora stopped him before he could get outside.

"I have a big to-do list, Nora."

"I just wanted to talk to you about the morning activities since I don't think I'll see you before my shift ends."

"Can't we debrief at home?"

She dropped her chin and stared at him through narrowed eyes. "What's wrong?"

"Nothing's wrong. I have things to do. That's it."

"Is it Sabrina? You heard about her and Dylan, didn't you?"

This little nugget of information shifted his focus. "What about Sabrina and Dylan?"

She sucked in a breath through her teeth. "Oh, man. You didn't hear about them?"

Obviously, the big news was that Sabrina and Dylan were together. He wasn't surprised she had moved on to someone else. Maybe he was slightly perturbed that it was Dylan, her ex, that she had sworn she had no feelings for anymore when she and Brady had first gotten together.

"I hope he makes her happier than he did the first time around. She used to tell me about all the annoying things he would do."

"She's pregnant," Nora blurted. "They're having a shotgun wedding at the end of the month."

Brady felt like he had been punched in the stomach and actually stumbled back a step. "What? A baby? A wedding?"

Nora placed a hand on his shoulder. "I'm

sorry. I didn't mean to drop that in your lap like this."

"Who did you hear it from?"

She dropped her hand. "Blair ran into Dylan's mom yesterday and she was complaining about having so much to do in such a short time. Not only did she have to help them plan a wedding, but she needed to prepare for becoming a grandma for the first time."

Three months. They had been broken up for three months and Sabrina was already getting married and having a baby. He tried to remember the last time he had run into her. There was so much going on at the inn, he hadn't been hanging out in town much. Last summer, Sabrina had visited him whenever she could, but since the breakup, he hadn't seen her at the Seasons Inn at all.

"I don't know what to say."

Nora was beside herself. "I thought that was why you looked so stressed. It's pretty hard to put you in a bad mood. I figured you must have heard since they're clearly not trying to hide it."

Did he really care what Sabrina did? He couldn't answer that.

"Hey, guys," Quinn interrupted. "I don't know why we decided to have some kind of intense conversation in the middle of the lobby, but we need to either take this into the office or move along."

Nora huffed. "Jeez, Quinn. Can you be a tiny bit sympathetic for once in your life?"

"What do I need to be sympathetic about? You're standing in the lobby of our inn, where guests get their first impression, having an obviously personal conversation. I don't care what it's about. Sorry if you're having a bad day, Brady, but can you please just have this chat in private?"

Getting into this with Quinn was the last thing Brady wanted. "I'm going to check on the van. I can't talk about this or anything right now."

Sabrina was getting married and having Dylan's baby. Brady must be living in some kind of alternate universe. Sabrina had never talked about wanting kids. When they were together, it hadn't come up. They didn't even talk about marriage. Goodness, no wonder she broke up with him. Had he even seen a future with her? She probably questioned that as well.

"Good afternoon, Brady," Maureen greeted him as soon as he stepped outside. She was one of his favorite people. He couldn't be in a bad mood when he was around Maureen.

"How's it going, Mo?"

"Living the dream, and the dream just got upgraded to a penthouse suite now that you're here," she replied.

She was the positivity he needed at the moment. She had worked for the Seasons Inn for as long as Brady could remember, and she always acted like it was the greatest thing she could be doing. "You always know the right thing to say."

"That sounds better than always saying the wrong thing!"

Brady had to laugh. Maureen had the right attitude. Focus on the good and enjoy the moment. That was what Brady was going to do. He was happy for Sabrina and Dylan. They had figured out how to make things work and were about to embark on this big beautiful adventure together. Good for them. As for Alexa, the real reason he had looked upset to his sister, he needed to appreciate the time he had with her. Better to know someone wonderful for a short period of time than to never know them at all. That was the perspective he needed to take. She might only be here for a brief time, but why not hang out in the penthouse of life until she had to go? That was what Maureen would do. He was sure of it.

"Can I get the keys to the van? I need to make sure it's ready for a trip into town." He didn't drive the van to excursions, since they had a driver for that, but he was in charge of making sure it had a full tank of gas and was clean and ready for guests.

"Oh, excellent." Maureen opened the valet

box in search of the keys for the inn's passenger van. She pulled them off the hook reserved for them. "The guests are going to love it downtown. You've got such a gorgeous day to make the trip. Be sure to tell them about the sodas at Cooper's."

Cooper's Pharmacy and Soda Fountain was always a highlight of a trip into town for Brady. Besides being a fully functional pharmacy, they served up the best old-fashioned sodas and milkshakes. It was always a special treat on a hot summer day. "Good call. I will definitely recommend that they make a stop there."

Brady was going to show Alexa everything he could squeeze in during her visit. If there wasn't a chance she could come back, he wanted her to do and see as much as possible. He was going to see to it that Apple Hollow would always hold a special place in her heart.

Nora stepped outside. "I let him know he's the worst."

"You didn't have to do that. It's fine. I'm guessing he hasn't heard the town gossip because he never leaves that counter, so he had no idea why he might need to be a little gentler."

"If anyone should be able to relate, it's him. That's what I told him."

Quinn's high-school sweetheart was supposed to have been the one. He'd had every intention of marrying her, but one day, she took off and never came back. Quinn didn't talk about it, but it was most likely the biggest reason he was obsessed with the inn. The inn could never leave him.

"I'm not upset. Sabrina and I were not meant to be. We never talked about getting married. We were content with the status quo until she wasn't. She wanted more and Dylan is clearly ready for that, so I'm fine."

"I'm sorry I didn't tell you yesterday."

Brady pulled his sister in for a hug. "Don't worry about it." He let her go. "By the way, the kayaking tours went great this morning. I do think that if we're going to have two groups, we should consider age groups. Maybe one for the younger guests and one for our sixty-plus."

"Oh, please don't do that!" Maureen interjected. "We seniors love it when we get a chance to mingle with the younger people. That's how we stay young. If I was stuck with a bunch of old people all the time, I'd be bummed."

"Good point. Ignore the age-group idea."

Nora loved Maureen as much as Brady did. "I want to be you when I grow up, Mo," she said. "You have the best way of looking at things."

"You're going to do just fine being you when you're my age. You are special, Nora Seasons. You spread joy around this place every day."

Nora pressed her hand over her heart. "Thanks.

You have no idea how much I needed to hear that today. Sometimes I wonder if I do."

"Why? What's going on?" Brady asked. He'd been so wrapped up in himself, he hadn't paid attention to Nora's mood.

"Ugh, I thought the friendly company of a nice guy was what Ms. Fox needed to make her vacation one to remember. I had such a good feeling about Mr. Leroy, but I talked to him today and he was *so* rude. The more I listened to him, the less I wanted him anywhere near Ms. Fox. She is so sweet, and I wasted so much time pushing a guy on her who was not worthy."

Finally, she saw what he saw. "I'm not going to say I told you so, but..."

Nora scowled at him. "Don't you dare. What I can't figure out is why she seemed to be into him the other day. There's no way she would find a man like him attractive. Not based on the impression he made today."

"I have been around the two of them plenty, and she is not into him. She has seen him as the guy you saw today the entire time."

"But I told you I heard her talking about someone she obviously had a crush on. If you had seen the way her face lit up while she was talking to her friend... I really thought I had done something good."

Nora's heart was so big. She loved love, and

wanted everyone to have it in their lives. "I spoke with her today. She couldn't say enough good things about her vacation, especially all of the fun things you set up for her. You did a fantastic job making her vacation special."

"Maybe that's enough," Nora said, and it hit home for Brady. Maybe what they had was enough. Maybe fate had brought her to the Seasons Inn to help him write his business plan and so he could make her smile the way she had with her friend on the phone. That had to be enough. Any more than that was asking too much.

CHAPTER NINE

ALEXA CHECKED HER makeup in the mirror one more time. She rubbed her finger over her right eyelid. She didn't need so much eye shadow—this was an afternoon trip into town to do some shopping, not some date night.

Why was it so hard to keep her cool? Whenever she thought about being around Brady, she got those anxious butterflies. Looking good for him was becoming a thing. It was silly and pointless, but she still had put on four different outfits before settling on a hot-pink cap-sleeved knit romper. Pink was a good color for her and this screamed comfortable and casual.

She dabbed on some light lip gloss and tossed it in her bag in case she needed a touch-up later. Not because she'd be doing anything with her lips, like kissing Brady's. That would not be happening. Rationally, she knew that. He had basically admitted at lunch today that his interest was a sales technique. She planned to be more business-minded moving forward. She was here for a vacation and to get more information on the inn's financial status, as well as gauge the owner's interest in taking on investors. Brady's dad wasn't interested in investors, but he had admitted he wasn't going to be around much longer, so it was time to find out how Brady and his siblings, who would be taking over, felt about it.

Everyone going into town was supposed to meet in the lobby at two thirty. Alexa noticed a few familiar faces. James and Cate were without their children. Maeve and Nathan from the bonfire were waiting by the oversize chairs. Maeve flashed Alexa her megawatt smile. There was a family with three little kids and a young couple Alexa didn't remember seeing around waiting as well.

The front door opened and Brady came striding in. His sunglasses dangled from a strap around his neck, just like the first time she'd laid eyes on him. His gaze locked on her almost immediately and those dimples in his cheeks made an appearance. Her jitters were back and it was as if the rest of the people in the lobby disappeared.

"He's dreamy, isn't he?"

Alexa hadn't noticed Maeve had moved to stand next to her. "Sorry?"

"Brady and those dimples. He's adorable. I know I'm a married woman, but I still have eyes."

Alexa wondered if it would bother her if her husband walked over to James and commented that way about Nora Seasons. But Maeve didn't seem the type to ever be concerned her husband would find anyone more attractive than her. Alexa had always been worried about that when she was married. Maybe that was why her comment irked Alexa so much.

Thankfully, Brady started calling out names to make sure everyone was there. Alexa wasn't sure what she could even say about him to someone else. She feared if she allowed herself to talk about him, she would give herself away as totally infatuated.

Everyone was accounted for, so they headed outside to board the twelve-passenger transport van. Alexa waited at the back of the line. When she got on, there were only two open seats next to one another in the front. She sat down next to the window, leaving Brady nowhere to sit but next to her.

"Are you ready to see downtown Apple Hollow?"

"I think so," she replied, self-conscious of the fact that their legs were touching.

"I know that New York City is the king of the big cities, but I would dare to say Apple Hollow is the queen of small towns. If you ever imagined living in a small town, moving to Apple Hollow will be hard to resist."

"You're really hyping it up. I hope you haven't oversold it or I'm going to be very disappointed."

"I promise you won't be disappointed. I will even give you a personal tour so you see all the best parts, if you'd like."

"Oh, I was planning on walking aimlessly around the market by myself."

He smirked at her playful banter. "I love that you are so funny."

His compliment caught her off guard. It had been a while since someone positively acknowledged her sense of humor. Brett had acted like she no longer had one.

"Really? You think I'm funny?"

"Of course I do," he replied, as if she was strange for asking. "I mean, not as funny as me, but you're pretty hilarious."

She wanted to balk at that, but he was the funnier of the two of them. "Fine, you may give me a tour of your tiny, little small town and I will decide for myself if it deserves to be the queen of small towns."

His dimples were even cuter up close and personal. "Oh, it does. Just you wait."

The inn wasn't far from the downtown area. The driver pulled into a large field that had been converted into a makeshift parking lot. The town's green hosted the farmer's market and was on the west side of Main Street in front of the historic Apple Hollow Library. There were also plenty of shops and restaurants along Main Street for the guests to visit. Brady stood up in the aisle and pulled some papers out of his clipboard.

"I have maps for everyone. On the other side is a list of all the vendors and which booth they are in on the green. The van returns to the inn at five. Please meet back here at least fifteen minutes before then."

As everyone debarked, they all took maps and went on their merry way. Brady and Alexa were quickly left alone.

"I didn't realize we were going to get maps. I guess I wouldn't have been roaming aimlessly. Maybe I don't need you after all." She folded her map in half and fanned herself with it.

He snatched it away from her. "Nope. You're coming with me. I would never forgive myself if I didn't make sure you saw all the hidden gems this place has to offer."

She followed him, surprised at how good he was at making her feel like he wanted to spend time with her. She was keeping it cool, going with the flow, not taking things too seriously. Everything she had coached herself to do in the mirror before she left.

"Where to first?" she asked, catching up to walk beside him.

He handed her the map back. "First, we go to Cooper's for an old-fashioned soda."

Main Street in Apple Hollow embodied everything she would expect from a small town in New England. It was something straight out of a storybook. The street was lined with colonial-style buildings. Colorful clapboard exteriors and steeply pitched roofs were adorned with white trim. Each building had its own unique character. Some of the stores had vintage wood signs hanging above the doors. Hanging baskets of vibrant red, yellow, and purple flowers hung from the light posts.

The sidewalks were narrow but well-maintained. These were nothing like the bustling sidewalks in downtown Manhattan. Here, everyone moved at a much slower pace and there was plenty of space between pedestrians.

There was a cozy little bookshop and a bakery that Alexa almost couldn't resist because of the scent of blueberry muffins that wafted out as they passed it.

"Trust me," Brady said, taking her by the hand as she drifted toward the baked goods displayed in the window. "Cooper's first."

On the corner of Main and Maple, a retro stamped tin sign hung on a pole protruding from the storefront of Cooper's Pharmacy and Soda Fountain. A picture of a milkshake was posted on the door.

"My friend Maureen back at the inn told me I should make sure I bring people here."

Alexa remembered Maureen from when she arrived at the Seasons Inn. "Maureen seems awesome. I think I should find out more about her because I think I want to be like her when I grow up," she said, taking a seat on one of the stools at the soda counter.

"That is exactly what my sister said today! Everyone wants to be Maureen. She's the best, and she knows what's best here in Apple Hollow."

"What would she order if she were here?" Alexa picked up a sticky, plastic-covered menu. They had a huge selection of flavors under Sodas and Phosphates.

Brady grabbed his own menu and perused it for a moment. "I can tell you that I am a big fan of the black-and-white, but I think Maureen would tell you to order with your heart. Whatever you decide to pick, you'll love."

"I don't want to be boring and get a root-beer float, so I think I'll try the pink lime rickey."

"How very old-fashioned soda of you. You're gonna love it."

An older gentleman with snow-white hair came over to take their order. He was totally dressed for the part, with a white button-down short-sleeved shirt and a little black bow tie under a red apron with the Cooper's Pharmacy and Soda Fountain logo on it.

While he made their drinks, Brady spun around on his stool and faced the rest of the store. "Do you know why pharmacies were home to soda shops back in the day?"

"I'm not sure—please enlighten me."

"People used to come here to get their medicine, and what better way than in a fizzy drink?"

"Ah, the old a-spoonful-of-sugar-helps-the-medicine trick."

Brady winked and gave her a nod. "Pharmacists and their science backgrounds would create tonics and mix in medicine or elixirs. They'd use the sweet syrups from sodas to make it go down a little easier. People would gather here to get their prescriptions and socialize at the soda counter. It was a much more wholesome gathering space than the bar farther down the street."

Alexa loved how Brady didn't just visit places, he got to know the history behind them and was always happy to share what he learned with someone else. When their drinks arrived, Alexa was not disappointed. The sweet mix of berries and citrus danced on her tongue. If this was only the first stop, she couldn't wait to see what else Brady had in store for her.

They spent the next two hours popping into a local art gallery, taste-testing a myriad of maple-infused treats, touring the oldest church in the county, walking through the exhibits at the Apple Hollow Historical Society, and checking out what all the amazing vendors were selling at the green.

The green was centrally located on Main Street in front of the library. Brady explained how it was the heart of Apple Hollow, the site of all major town events. There were more than a dozen canopy tents set up in rows across the green today. Local farmers were selling fresh produce, their tables loaded up with sweet corn and baskets of berries, cherries, and peaches. One woman was selling brown eggs and a variety of cheeses Alexa had never heard of before.

Brady led her to a table that held buckets of colorful flowers for people to build their own bouquets.

"If it isn't my favorite customer," the woman behind the table said as they approached. She was probably the same age as Maureen. She had jet-black hair and wore large round-frame glasses. "How are you, Brady dear?"

"I'm amazing, Miss Matilda. Even better now that I've found your booth."

"This boy is one of the good ones," Matilda said to Alexa. "He usually likes to visit me at least once a month at my shop around the corner."

Alexa could only imagine all the pretty girls Brady had bought flowers for over the years. The thought made the pink lime rickey sour her stomach.

"I bet he buys a lot of flowers while he's running around charming the socks off all the ladies in town."

Matilda shook her head. "Oh, he's a charmer, but this guy only buys flowers for his mother. She raised him right."

Brady's cheeks turned pink. He cleared his throat. "This is Alexa. She's a guest at the inn and we have become friends."

"It's nice to meet you. Let me guess your flower," Matilda said, getting off the stool she had been perched on.

Alexa gave Brady a quizzical look, and he explained, "Matilda has a gift of matching the flower to the person. She knows what you're going to love before you do."

Go with the flow, Alexa told herself. It was exciting to see what Matilda came up with. The woman began grabbing different stems and piling them together into a beautiful bouquet brimming with roses, orchids, lilies, and lush greenery.

Alexa's mouth hung open as Matilda wrapped

them up. "How did you know purple was my favorite color?"

"It's your aura, dear. Purple means you are wise, intellectual, and independent. Light purple is also connected to lighthearted romantic energy." She smiled at Brady. "But darker purples sometimes relate with a little bit of frustration and sadness. I sense you might be trying to overcome some of that so I put both shades in here."

Alexa felt a chill go down her spine. "How much do I owe you?"

Matilda waved her off. "Oh, a friend of Brady's gets the first bouquet on the house. You come back next time and I'll let you pay."

Alexa got a little choked up at her kindness. Brady tugged her along, waving goodbye to his friend. "Thank you, Matilda." As they made their way down the aisle, he said, "She really believes she is magical. I think she's the reason my sister also thinks she has superpowers."

"Well, Matilda was freakishly accurate." Alexa was still feeling off-kilter after their exchange. "What superpower does your sister think she has?"

"Promise not to laugh?"

"No," she replied honestly, which in turn made him laugh.

"Fine. My sister thinks that she is a matchmaker. It might be why you found yourself on several excursions with Richard."

Alexa widened her eyes. "Your sister was trying to match me up with Richard?"

Brady cringed. "Yeah, she doesn't always get it right like Matilda."

Alexa burst out laughing. "No, she absolutely does not."

After walking around the rest of the market, they took a seat on a bench under a large shade tree. There was the quintessential small-town gazebo next to the library. A man with a guitar stood inside it, entertaining the crowd with his songs. Apple Hollow was without a doubt the queen of small towns.

"You know what I love about this town more than anything?" Brady asked, setting the gift bag of jams he'd bought to take home to his family on the other side of him.

Alexa was truly curious because she wasn't sure she could put her finger on just one thing. She had loved every single aspect of it. "Tell me," she said, shifting in her seat so she could face him better.

"I've lived here my whole life, been to all the places we visited today, and still there's always something new. You'd think, oh, this is a small town, you can see everything in a day. That has to be so boring after a while. But that's not true.

The people who live here pride themselves on being innovative and find ways to create new experiences all the time. Every season brings with it different activities and novelties. I love that I know this place so well, but I'll never know what's coming next at the same time."

"I love that. When you put it that way, it makes New York seem like the boring place to live."

"I warned you. Once you experience Apple Hollow, you might not want to leave."

She knew he was saying it to be funny, but it felt very similar to their conversation at lunch. As much as she was enjoying her time here, she was leaving on Sunday. It was simply the way it was. There was no changing her life, and her life was in New York.

"Thank you for sharing your hometown with me. I really enjoyed it," she said, attempting to go back to playing it cool.

"You are very welcome." His brown eyes sucked her in. For a second she thought he was going to lean over and kiss her. Instead, Brady broke the spell and glanced down at his watch. "We should probably head back to the van. Our driver waits for no one, including me." He stood up and held out a hand to help Alexa to her feet. He was always so thoughtful like that. Brady was a true gentleman.

Everyone made it back to the van in time.

Most of the guests had bags of goodies they had purchased in town. Alexa rested her flowers on her lap as she waited for everyone to board.

"Those are gorgeous," Maeve said as she passed by. "Did a special someone buy those for you?"

Alexa didn't like what she was trying to imply. "Actually, the woman selling them liked me so much, she gave them to me."

The look of surprise on Maeve's face was satisfying. She really thought she had been onto something. Brady and Alexa were simply becoming friends, like he had told Matilda. There was no reason to think anything else.

When they got back to the inn, Brady asked Alexa to wait for him. She hung back as everyone else went in and Brady and the van driver chatted for a second.

"Sorry," he said as he jogged over to her, carrying his bag of jams.

"It's fine. Thanks again for everything."

"You don't have to thank me. I love showing off Apple Hollow. I bought you something to remember my little town by when you go back to the big city."

Alexa's heart thudded hard in her chest as he reached into his bag and pulled out a postcard. "I know some people have been giving you a hard time for not getting a picture of either of the moose you've seen while you've been here, but I thought maybe you could use this to show your friends back home what you saw. Or it can simply be a reminder of your time here and that you're always welcome back." He turned the card over so she could see the photo of the moose with Greetings From Apple Hollow written across the top.

Alexa took the postcard and was overwhelmed with emotion for a second time in two days. She needed a moment to compose herself enough to respond. "When did you get this?"

"While you were using the restroom at Cooper's. I saw it and knew I had to get it for you." He held open the door to the inn for her.

The moose looked exactly like the two she had seen. It wasn't as if she would ever be able to forget this experience, because her trip and the people she had met were totally unforgettable. Especially the man standing in front of her.

"I love it," she said, stepping through the doorway. He made it very hard to not fall head over heels for him. Brady was one of the good ones, just as Matilda had said. "I'm glad you're letting me do something nice for you for once. We're still on for tonight, right?"

Alexa followed Brady's gaze to the front desk. Quinn was helping a guest and Nora was busy on her computer. His siblings hadn't noticed the two of them yet.

Brady lowered his voice, speaking close to her ear. "I'm counting on you to help me write a business plan that's going to blow my dad away. Seven, right?"

"Seven o'clock in the Garden Suite. But I should warn you, we might need more than one night. There's very likely some research we'll need to do based on your ideas."

"Are you telling me there's going to be homework associated with this thing?"

Alexa pressed her lips together and nodded.

"Well, tonight, I'll bring the ideas, you bring the things you need to make a plan. I don't know what that would be, but I assume you do."

Alexa let out an amused laugh. She could see why he needed help. Brady was a doer. He worked hard and could tell someone why doing something in a new way would be better than the way they were currently doing it. What he needed was a numbers guy—or gal, in this case. He needed someone to help him figure out how much all his good ideas were going to cost and who was his best bet to make them happen.

"My laptop will be ready to do lots of internet searches," she assured him.

"If you'd like, I could take your flowers and

have someone put them in a vase for you. They can deliver them to your room."

"That's kind of you." Alexa handed him the bouquet. He anticipated needs and often took care of them himself. How was she going to find someone like him in New York?

"Later," he said, heading in the opposite direction of her elevator. As soon as she got to her room, she flopped on the couch and held the postcard to her chest. It wasn't fancy or expensive, but it was thoughtful and showed he truly cared.

Her phone rang, ending her good mood. It was Jordan calling, which was normal on a workday after five o'clock, but not when she was on vacation. She answered it, even though she could have let it go to voice mail. He wouldn't be bothering her unless it was important.

"Hey, Jordan, what's going on?"

"The Steel Masters project is dead, Alexa. Why do you have to be out of town when the project falls apart? I need you and you're not here."

She got up off the couch and went right to the desk with her laptop on it. She'd said she wasn't going to work, but this was an emergency. "It's not going to fall apart. Tell me what happened and I'll fix it with you."

"It's not fixable. It's done. They sold to someone else this morning before they even announced they were going to take bids." It didn't matter why it had happened, or how. Steel Masters was off the list. "We need something else to present to Roger next week. Neil said you were checking out the property you're vacationing at. What about that?"

Alexa suddenly felt very protective of the Seasons Inn. She had spent the first few days gathering some intel and documenting her findings, but since getting to know Brady, she wasn't so keen on turning over any of the information to anyone. She would rather work the rest of this week looking for a different viable project to present by next week.

"I don't think discussing the inn is the way to go with this little time. I need you to see if we can push our presentation back to two weeks from today instead of one. Can you do that for me?"

"I can try. I think the inn is doable if we both work together. I started looking at it and it's owned by one family. How have they never taken an investor all this time? That piece of land is prime real estate."

Of course, he went looking for information on his own when he knew this was something she was working on. Alexa wasn't a fan of being untruthful. She prided herself on being honest in her business dealings. She was always upfront with Roger and the team. She never made promises to anyone from the companies that they were attempting to invest in, knowing Roger always did what was best for Roger.

"I think I can find us a better project."

"I like this one, Alexa. Your instincts are always good."

"Get me that extra time and I'll see what I can do."

They said their goodbyes and Alexa ended the call. Things were much more critical than they had been ten minutes ago. She had to figure out how to help Brady write a business plan to improve the inn, while at the same time figure out how to stop Roger from finding out that he could exploit them by either getting them to sell it to him, or allowing him to invest and take controlling interest.

Sometimes what Roger did was good for him *and* the business he was taking over. That could be true for the inn. She had overheard some workers talking about how there were some major electrical issues. The inn was old and even though things like the linens and the furniture were all top-notch, the bones of the building were beginning to show their age. Some major renovations were going to be needed soon.

Maybe Gatton Investments could invest in the

future of the Seasons Inn. Maybe Roger could help them update things and make a profit for them and him. Alexa wished she could believe that. She knew that if Roger found out there was this huge chunk of lakeside land up for grabs, he would snatch it up and sell it. The inn would be knocked down and there would be luxury condos in its place in no time.

She couldn't let that happen. Not to the inn and not to Brady.

CHAPTER TEN

BRADY MUST HAVE checked his watch a hundred times in the last hour. How could a minute go by so slowly? Sixty seconds was sixty seconds. How did it suddenly become longer than that?

When his watch finally said it was seven, he made his way to the Garden Suite. Brady was impressed with her room choice. The Garden Suite had spectacular views of the lake and a private balcony. She had excellent taste.

He had attempted to write down a few notes for her and for himself. He didn't want to forget anything and then have to come back to her later to ask her to add it to the plan. He wanted to get it right the first time. The proposal needed to be on his dad's desk ASAP. He was going to show Quinn that he was capable of not only thinking outside the box, but also following all of his dumb business rules.

Alexa answered her door before he could knock more than once. Maybe she was just as eager to see him again as he was to see her.

"Hi," she said, holding the door open wide and motioning for him to come in.

"Hi," he returned, reminding himself not to make this weird. He was in her room and they were going to work. They were friends. All of this was no big deal. "Have you been able to relax a little since dinner?"

"I took a shower and changed into comfortable clothing, if that's what you mean by relaxing," Alexa said. She was dressed in some pale pink shorts and a white T-shirt. Her hair was a little wet and she wasn't wearing any makeup. She still looked beautiful, maybe even more so.

"I think that counts. I am really sorry to ask you to do this for me. I know this is your downtime, your vacation away from stuff like this."

She shook her head. "Brady, I am happy to help. I promise you that I wouldn't do anything I didn't want to do on my vacation."

"Well, I did make you partner with Richard on two separate occasions, so..." She'd have to admit that he had her there.

"While that is true," she said, raising a finger to make a point, "I didn't know at the time that being his partner was something I didn't want to do. Believe me, if you ask me to partner with him again, I will refuse."

"Don't worry, that is never going to happen. Not as long as it's an activity run by me."

"Maybe you could mention to your sister that Richard and I are not a match. Or should I?"

"Oh, Nora has come to her senses. She had the privilege of seeing Richard's unpleasant side and decided she didn't want him anywhere near you. I think you're in the clear now."

"Thank goodness." She sighed with relief. "Are you ready to share your ideas with me so I can help you make them a reality?"

Her words were music to his ears. Brady had been ready ever since she offered to help. "I brought some notes that I jotted down on this napkin." He had been sitting in the kitchen when he realized he should come to this meeting a little prepared. Notes seemed like a good start.

The Garden Suite was one of the larger rooms at the inn. There was a sitting room and a separate bedroom with views of the lake. At the center of the sitting room was a comfortable couch upholstered in a soft sage-green fabric with a glass coffee table set in front of it. The flowers Matilda had picked for her sat in a vase next to her computer. On the other side of the coffee table were two ivory armchairs, positioned to encourage conversation. On the opposite wall from where Brady stood, French doors led to a private balcony that overlooked the grounds and offered a breathtaking view of the lake.

Alexa took a seat on the couch and reached

for the laptop that had been sitting on the coffee table. "Do you want to sit and look over your notes together?"

Brady was much too anxious to sit. "How about I read them off to you and we go from there?"

She motioned for him to proceed, watching him as he paced in front of the French doors.

"First thing, the inn is in desperate need of some upgrades, especially electrical. I think it would be attractive to guests if there were more outlets in the rooms and if they were multifunctional. You know, like the type that are outfitted with USB ports."

Alexa adjusted to sit cross-legged on the couch with her computer on her lap. Her eyebrows pinched together. "How desperate is the need for an electrical upgrade?"

"I heard my brother and dad talking about it the other day. Quinn was pretty hot about it. Breakers keep getting tripped and our head of maintenance said there's nothing he can really do to fix it."

"Are we talking about the whole inn needing to be rewired? New circuit boards being put in?"

Brady rubbed the back of his neck. She had questions he didn't have answers for. "I think I need to put that on my homework list."

"Agreed. You need to figure out if they're

already looking to spend money on fixing the bigger issue before we ask them to spend more money on something that isn't reasonable if they don't do the bigger thing first."

That made sense. Maybe the outlets weren't the best place to start. "What if we scrap the outlet upgrade for now and focus on something that I think will drive up revenue rather than cost us money?"

"I think you would be showing me that you are a savvy businessman. What's your money-making idea?" Her fingers were poised over the keyboard ready to type whatever he was going to say next.

"I want to start an annual event called 'A Day at the Lake.'"

Alexa looked intrigued and started typing. "Tell me more."

A Day at the Lake was an idea that Brady had been trying to sell to his dad for a couple years. Just like the farmer's market brought out the community and poured money into the local businesses, he felt that an annual event at the lake could do the same thing. He even saw a future for it being seasonal, rather than annual.

Alexa typed as he explained his vision in as much detail as he could muster. She barely stopped him to ask questions. She just kept typing and nodding her head. Occasionally she would say something like "I like that" or "oh, that sounds cool."

When he had rattled off everything he could think of, she stopped and intertwined her fingers on top of her head. "I am completely in love with the idea of Seasons at the Lake sponsored by the Seasons Inn. I mean, it doesn't get any better than that to give you amazing branding options."

Brady gripped the back of the armchair. "You like it? You think this is something that could actually work?"

"We have a bunch of things to hammer out, that's for sure. You're going to need to be way more specific about some of these things you envision, but all in all, this is a fantastic idea. I don't know how your dad couldn't love it."

"Really?" Brady felt like he was ten feet tall. The validation she gave him was like finding fresh water on a deserted island. He had needed that.

"Really. I think we should start with summer. I feel like I can help the most with that one since I'm here now, during the summer. I could give feedback based on personal experience rather than just imagining it."

For the first time since he walked in the door, he felt like he needed to sit down. He stepped around the chair and plopped down into it. "Do you think it's something I'll be able to present to my dad this weekend?"

"You're going to have to make some calls and ask some questions around town. If we work really hard, it could be ready to present by the weekend."

"I'm ready if you are."

"Maybe we should order some room service first. I think I need some food to fuel my brain power."

"I could eat. Let me call the kitchen. If they know it's for me, we'll get it faster." Perks of being one of the Seasons.

Alexa got up and scanned the room-service menu, even though Brady tried to tell her that he could probably get her anything she wanted within reason. They ordered some food and a couple of sodas. Brady liked that she wasn't afraid to order some fried-chicken tenders with extra ranch on the side. Sabrina used to only eat salad and quinoa. There had been so many times he'd begged her to eat a cheeseburger, share a pizza with him, or indulge in something like chocolate cake or a milkshake from Cooper's. What kind of life was it to restrict yourself from enjoying some of the best foods the world had to offer?

"You good?" she asked, pulling him from his thoughts.

"Sorry." He didn't want to think about his ex or what she used to not eat, or how she was getting married or that she was having a baby. Although, he wondered if the baby would cause her to crave real food. "I'm just thinking about stuff that doesn't matter. Should we start planning while we wait for the food?"

Before Alexa could reply, her phone began dinging like it was being attacked by text messages. A barrage of seven, eight, nine, hit her phone. Alexa picked it up and scanned through them.

"Is everything okay? What was that all about?"

Frown lines etched her forehead. "It's stupid work issues. I know I shouldn't let work interfere with my vacation, but I really need to respond to these. Can you give me a minute?"

"Absolutely. Do what you need to do."

She texted back and forth with someone, her thumbs moving across her phone screen with incredible speed. He admired that she took her work seriously. She had to be good at her job if they were asking for her help while she was on vacation. He hoped she had good boundaries, but something told him that she would sacrifice her free time to take care of things at work.

"Sorry. I hate that I can't disconnect from everything back in New York. This is exactly why my husband left me. We'd be somewhere and I'd be on my phone while he sat there like you are, waiting for me to rejoin the conversation." She tossed her phone to the other side of the couch. "Except, oftentimes I didn't rejoin the conversation because work came first."

"It can be hard to balance. That's why I picked a job where I got to do the things I love at work, so I rarely have to choose between my responsibilities and recreation."

"You are superfortunate to get to do that. I hate that I always feel like I have to choose. Be successful at work, or have meaningful relationships and a life outside of work. It's always one or the other."

"I think you're looking at it the wrong way."

Alexa's brow furrowed. "What do you mean?"

"My dad has tried to instill in me and my brothers and sister that work should be what allows you to have a life, it shouldn't *be* your life. I don't think it should be an either-or situation."

Alexa leaned back in her seat. "I don't want it to be that way. It simply is. The only way I could have been the wife Brett wanted me to be was to quit my job. The only way to succeed at my job was to be a terrible wife."

"Can I make an objective observation?" She motioned for him to go ahead. "I have nothing to gain from what you do with your life, but it seems to me that you weren't eager to be the kind of wife Brett wanted you to be, but you aren't exactly happy being tied to your job twenty-four seven, either."

"You think I wanted my marriage to end?" Her back straightened and her tone shifted. "I thought Brett and I were going to be together forever. That was what I signed up for."

Brady put up his hands. "No, no. I don't think you wanted your marriage to fail. You do not like failing at things—I know that much about you. But I saw your face when you said 'the only way I could have been the wife Brett wanted was to quit my job.' I didn't get the sense that the wife he wanted was the same wife you wanted to be."

Alexa rubbed her eyes with the heels of her hands and let out an exasperated sigh. "I don't know. I can't even tell you you're wrong."

Brady stood up and stepped around the coffee table, taking a seat next to her on the couch. He hadn't intended to make her feel bad. He placed a hand on her knee. "Maybe what you need is to change how you're approaching this. Maybe it's not a choice between this part of your life or that one. Maybe you need to simply consider what makes you happy. And if neither of the two things you're choosing between make you happy, you need to change the options, not pick the lesser of the two evils."

She was quiet for a second. "Well, one of the options already took itself out of the running," she said sadly.

"If he couldn't help you figure this out, then he wasn't the right choice, anyway."

Alexa blew out a long breath. "It might hurt less if I could believe that."

Brady gave her knee a squeeze. "If it makes you feel any better, I just found out that my ex-girlfriend, who broke up with me three whole months ago, is getting married at the end of the month and having a baby. It was a double gut punch today."

"Oh, man." Alexa cringed. "We're both a couple of sad sacks, huh?"

"I've decided to look at it like this is proof that Sabrina and I weren't meant to be. I'm trying to live in the moment and appreciate all the good things in my life instead of dwelling on the bad."

Alexa tilted her head. "Can you teach me how to do that?"

"If I figure it out, I sure will. But why don't we focus on Seasons at the Lake because I think that is something we were both feeling pretty good about before we decided to drift down this sad path."

"Sorry, I didn't mean to change the vibe so much."

A knock at the door had them both jumping to

their feet. "I think we both need to eat and then the good vibes will be back in full force." The smile on her face told him she agreed.

They ate their after-dinner snack and brainstormed ideas for the summer version of Seasons at the Lake. Before they knew it, it was midnight. Brady had never had so much fun talking with someone as he did with Alexa. She had this way of listening to him and finding the right way to express his thoughts so they would make sense to someone else. She also had such good questions. Brady had a bunch of things to do for homework by the time they were wrapping up.

Alexa yawned and he knew that was his cue. "I need to let you get to bed. I have taken up enough of your time tonight."

"No, it was actually fun. In my line of work, I'm usually focused on all the things that are wrong with a business. It was nice to work on a way to build something up instead of tearing it down."

"I'm glad I could let you use your powers for good." Brady couldn't stop staring into her eyes. In this light and in a room filled with soft green accents, her eyes were like emeralds. How could someone not want to spend a lifetime looking at them? This Brett guy was an idiot.

"I'm scheduled for a yoga class in the morning." She cocked an eyebrow, perhaps waiting for him to say whether he was leading the activity.

"Not me. We have a very nice woman named Josie come in from town to lead yoga."

"In the afternoon, I have an archery lesson." She paused again.

"That's with me. I hope you're ready to see how Robin Hood-ish I can be."

"Can't wait." Her smile was broad. "And lastly, I will be going to something called Wickets and Wine. I am not sure what a wicket is, but I'm looking forward to the wine."

"That's not me, but I think I'm going to come play. My shift should be over by then. And a wicket is the little metal arch that you hit a croquet ball through. It's a very fun event that Ivy runs."

"I never realized those things had a name. Maybe after we hit our croquet balls through the wickets we can get together again to look at all the questions that needed a deeper dive," she offered.

Another evening like this sounded better than anything else Brady could be doing. "It's a date."

Alexa escorted him to the door. She held on to the doorknob with both hands and made him wish he didn't have to leave. "Until tomorrow."

"It's actually already tomorrow, so I guess it's more like 'until later today.'"

Her closed-mouth smile was so cute, he wanted to take a step closer and kiss her just to see if it would feel as amazing as he imagined it would. But she was a guest, leaving in a few days. If he started kissing her now, he'd probably feel a million times worse when she left. He stepped into the hall and gave her a little wave before striding down the hall with what was probably the most ridiculous lovestruck expression on his face. Why did the most incredible woman he'd ever met have to be from New York, and totally unattainable, at that? It was just his luck.

He got into the elevator and hit the button for the lobby. He didn't expect anyone to be around this late at night. Which is why he was surprised to see Quinn standing there when the elevator doors opened. His brother's face went from disinterested to confused to suspicious in the blink of an eye.

"What the heck were you doing upstairs at this time of night?"

CHAPTER ELEVEN

BRADY'S WORDS RAN through Alexa's head in the morning. During yoga, she kept thinking about how he had basically told her she shouldn't be choosing between two things she didn't love. She should be putting more energy into figuring out what made her happy instead.

Easier said than done.

There was one thing she knew for a fact, as she followed Josie's directions to go into a downward dog position: she did not love yoga. Being at the inn had opened her eyes to a lot of new things she could now say she liked and others she did not like. She definitely wanted to go four-wheeling again, and the idea of snowmobiling was also kind of intriguing. Although she couldn't be sure if it was the idea of riding a snowmobile or spending the day on the trails with Brady that was the most enticing. Actually, she knew it was the latter.

She had already googled some places she could take tennis lessons when she got home.

There was no way she was ever going to Wimbledon, but she might eventually get good enough to join a women's tennis league.

"Take a deep breath," Josie said. "And let it out slowly. We're going to go from downward-facing dog to a half-moon pose. This pose helps with balance and body awareness. Step your right foot to your right hand."

Alexa was suddenly reminded of being on that paddleboard her first full day at the inn. That seemed like so long ago. She really needed to give paddleboarding another chance. She needed to prove to herself that she could stand on that darn board before she left. She had loved being on the water. Surprisingly, it was one of the most relaxing things she had done.

"Move your right hand forward about twelve inches but keep your fingertips on the ground. Good." Josie was moving around the group, helping those who were struggling a bit. "Bring your left hand to your left hip as you straighten your right leg and lift your left leg parallel to the floor."

Alexa struggled to keep all the directions straight as she focused on not falling on her face. She turned her head to see if the woman in front of her had it figured out. She was bent over at the waist, balanced on her right foot with her left leg parallel to the ground. Her right hand was still touching the ground with her fingertips. When Alexa tried to do the same thing, it felt like she was using every muscle in her body.

"Slowly turn your chest to face the left, twisting your torso and hips. Reach your top hand to the sky."

If Alexa had been doing this over water, she was sure she was seconds away from getting wet.

"Focus on your breathing and clear your mind," Josie said from beside her mat. "You've got this. Breathe and concentrate on your body doing what you want it to do."

Alexa inhaled and exhaled. She stopped worrying about how many times she had fallen that week and told her body to get into the pose. She turned her chest and reached her left hand to the sky.

"Great job," Josie said.

There was nothing better than succeeding at something she thought she couldn't do. Alexa smiled as she felt her body engaging all those muscles the way it was supposed to.

When the class was over, she used a towel to wipe the sweat from her forehead and neck. Perhaps she didn't dislike yoga as much as she did at the beginning. She'd have to take another class before she left, to make sure.

She turned in her yoga mat and picked up her

personal belongings from the picnic table Josie had set up as her check-in and check-out desk. Out of habit, she checked her phone and regretted it right away.

There were two missed calls from Jordan and a bunch of texts. She had told him last night to give her some time to figure this out, but he was incapable of doing that. Thankfully, he had managed to get them another week before they presented a new opportunity to Roger. She wished Neil hadn't told Jordan about the inn, but she couldn't blame him. It wasn't like Neil would know Alexa had a change of heart after meeting the family that owned the property.

She found a shade tree to sit under and hit the screen to return his call. He answered on the second ring.

"Why are you not near your phone? I know you're on vacation but don't you keep your phone on you?" he said.

"No, Jordan. I don't keep my phone on me all the time when I'm on vacation. I'm doing things that make my vacation more enjoyable and they require me to put my phone away so I can fully participate in them."

"Whatever. I've been doing some digging into public records and that inn you're visiting is in a bit of financial trouble. Looks like they took out a big loan about four years ago and interest rates were not good. They're basically only paying off the interest. What have you managed to find out on your side? Does it seem like they might need more money soon? Maybe there's an operational issue? The property is worth a ton. Any idea if they have another source of money over there?"

The thought of sharing anything she knew about the Seasons Inn with Jordan made her sick to her stomach. Telling him about all the issues would be betraying Brady. She couldn't do it.

"I'm still trying to find another project to pitch."

"What else is there to pitch, Alexa?" His voice was strained with anxiety. Jordan was constantly in fear of displeasing Roger and losing his job. He was stressed to the point that Alexa was sure he was going to give himself a heart attack one of these days.

"What about that tech company we talked about last month?"

"That's not as good as the property up there."

Jordan was no dummy. He did his job just as well as Alexa. The truth was Gavin Seasons had taken out a loan that he couldn't find a way to pay off *and* his inn needed some major renovations that, if not done, would start impacting business. Unless he had a money tree hiding among the maple trees, he was going to need to take on an investor to help.

As much as she'd like to help them find someone who could get them out of trouble, she wasn't sure Roger would choose to leave them alone after that. Roger had a tendency to see nothing but dollar signs. The land that the Seasons Inn was on was worth a fortune. All this lakeside acreage was more than desirable. Roger could tear down the inn, divide up the land, sell it in chunks, and make more money than he would know what to do with.

"You are the smartest person in our group. If you had the instinct to check out this inn, you need to trust that. You are usually right. Find a reason for them to need Roger's help and let's brainstorm all the things Roger can do once he takes control to make him ridiculous amounts of money."

Usually that would get Alexa's adrenaline pumping, but right now she felt numb. How was she going to protect this place? Was it too late?

She hung up with Jordan and went to her room to shower. What should have been a relaxing experience turned into thinking about all the companies she'd had a hand in destroying over the last five years. She had told Brady last night that she spent her days focusing on what was wrong with a business. The truth was she made plans that helped Roger either dismantle businesses or transform them into something else completely.

How many others like Gavin Seasons had she done in? How many of their mistakes had she exploited? How many of them had children who imagined one day running the family business, before Gatton Investments took over and sold their dream in pieces to the highest bidder?

That was when it hit her. Brady was right: her job didn't make her happy. She had spent the last few years choosing between two things that didn't fill her with joy. The job had somehow become the lesser of the two evils. She wasn't ready to be a stay-at-home mom so she put all her energy into working for a man who had never helped build anything. Roger Gatton only knew how to tear things apart for profit.

This revelation was mind-blowing. It was possibly life-changing. It was time for Alexa to figure out if there was a third option—one that made her happy. She hoped that it wasn't too elusive, and she might be stuck in this life that didn't feel right.

When she arrived at her archery lesson, the first thing she noticed was that Brady opted to wear a shirt today, which was actually kind of disappointing. Alexa felt like Maeve, ogling the poor guy who was simply trying to do his job. He still looked cute, though. He had his sunglasses on and his clipboard in his hand.

His face broke into the biggest smile when

he finally looked up from his list and saw her standing on the edge of the group that had gathered for the lesson.

"Welcome to archery. When I call your name, just let me know you're here so I know if we're missing anyone. Alexa Fox?" He pretended to scan the crowd as if he didn't know who she was.

"Here," she called out, raising her hand.

"Oh, there you are. Welcome, Ms. Fox." He put a check by her name and called the next name on the list.

Alexa realized in that moment how very fond of him she had become. Just the thought of him made her happy. Seeing him in person gave her a rush of excitement.

"Richard Leroy?"

"Here." Richard, on the other hand, sucked all the excitement out of her.

Alexa decided she'd better take a look around. She was not going to be Richard's buddy for archery, so she needed to find someone else immediately. She noticed Cate and James were there, as was their daughter, Kayleigh. No Donovan. That meant Kayleigh needed a partner. Alexa was going to suggest that they be buddies. She started moving closer to where they were standing.

Brady finished reading the names off his list and set down his clipboard. "Excellent. I am so glad you all could join me today. As you can see, we have several targets set up. I'm going to ask that you get into groups of four. If you need some help finding a group, give me a holler and I'll help you find one."

Alexa jumped in front of Cate. "I don't see your son. Do you guys need a fourth?"

Startled, Cate took a second before she realized who was asking. "Oh, Alexa. Absolutely, please be in our group."

"Oh, good! That means Brady will come over and help us the most," Kayleigh said.

Feeling her cheeks flush, Alexa ignored the comment and followed them to their target. Each group had a basket of arrows and two bows.

"Have you ever done this before?" Cate asked.

Alexa shook her head. "No. I did watch *The Hunger Games*, though. That made it look pretty easy. How about you?"

"I do some bowhunting, but this is different," James replied.

"Kayleigh did some archery at camp, didn't you, honey?"

"Yeah, when I was like ten. I don't remember how to do it, though."

"I'm sure Brady will show us exactly what to do," Alexa said.

"I'm sure he will." Kayleigh's eyebrows lifted

as she smirked. "He'll probably spend the whole time with our group."

"Stop it, Kayleigh," her mom scolded.

"Why do you think he's going to be over here all the time?" Alexa asked, feeling as if she needed to take control of the situation.

"Um, because he's in love with you," Kayleigh said, like it was the most obvious thing ever.

Alexa knew her face was bright red but she tried to sound as if she had no idea what the teen was talking about. "That is absolutely *not* true."

"Okay, can I get everyone's attention?" Brady shouted, causing all heads to turn his way. "I'm going to demonstrate for everyone and go over some safety rules, then you'll all get a turn to take your best shot."

Alexa's head was spinning. Kayleigh's assertion that Brady was in love with her was one of the silliest things she'd ever heard. It was such a high-school thing: a boy talks to a girl and clearly that means he's in love with her. Kayleigh just didn't understand that a man and a woman could simply be friendly. No one was in love.

Brady showed everyone how to place their arrow on their bow, point it at the target, pull back, and release—and as usual, he was an expert. He hit the bull's-eye with ease. A couple of people had questions and he answered them before saying that the groups should all wait until everyone had finished shooting to go and retrieve their arrows.

James went first in their group. He picked up the bow and placed the arrow's nock on the bowstring between the two rubber rings. He then demonstrated to his daughter how to pull back and keep the arrow level. James hit the target in the outermost ring on the right side. Kayleigh went next and the arrow hit the ground about three feet in front of the target.

"You have to pull back a little more," James instructed.

Alexa wasn't feeling too confident when her turn came. She looked around for Brady. He was all the way down the line, helping an older woman keep her bow steady before letting the arrow fly.

She wanted to get Kayleigh's attention and say "see?" Brady helped everyone and spent time making sure all the guests were having a good time and understood how to do the activity correctly. He wasn't showing Alexa any special treatment.

The four of them took turns shooting at the target. Alexa had successfully hit the target every time but the arrow only stuck in place twice. The other two arrows ricocheted off. She was having fun, though. James and Cate were encouraging and everyone was excited when one of them hit the target.

About halfway through the activity, Alexa realized Brady hadn't stopped by their group to check on them. Not even once. He had gone down the line and right before he got to them, he skipped to the last group in the row.

Alexa had thought Kayleigh was silly to think he'd be hanging around them the whole time, but she had believed he would come over to talk to her. The fact that he almost seemed to be avoiding them bothered her. Had something happened? The guilt she felt over talking to Jordan about the Seasons Inn began to creep back over her.

"Brady! I need your help!" Kayleigh shouted after her arrow landed on the ground in front of the target.

With a tiny bit of hesitation, he came over. "How can I help, Miss Kayleigh?"

"I stink at this and my dad stinks at coaching me."

"Kayleigh!" her mom reprimanded. "Your dad was being very helpful. Be nice."

"Let me see you shoot one," Brady said, folding his arms across his chest. Alexa forced herself to look away and not stare at his tanned forearms. He hadn't acknowledged that she was standing a couple feet away.

Kayleigh shot an arrow and it hit the very bottom of the target.

"Where were you aiming when you shot it?" Brady asked.

"The bull's-eye," she replied, as if it was obvious.

"Aim higher. Aim for the red ring and pull it back about one inch farther than you did the last time."

She reloaded, and James said, "That's what I told her to do the last time."

"Brady is more specific," she argued. She did as Brady suggested and her arrow hit just below the bull's-eye. It was her best shot of the day. Kayleigh threw her hands up in the air and walked over to high-five Brady.

"Nice one. Keep doing that and you'll be hitting all bull's-eyes." He started to back away as though he was going to leave, but Kayleigh stopped him. "Alexa needs some help, too. Her arrows just bounce off the target. Can you do something?"

Embarrassment heated her cheeks as Alexa dared glance in his direction. That hesitation was back in his step, but he rejoined their group. "Sure. Let's see you shoot an arrow."

"It's fine. I'm sure I'll get it eventually." She didn't want to make him stay if he wanted to go. She hated that it seemed like he wanted to go.

Finally, he cracked a tiny smile. "Alexa, show me what you've got."

She walked over to the basket of arrows and picked one up. There was no way she was going to do a good job with the four of them staring at her. She pulled back on the bowstring and released the arrow. Just like it had the last two times, it bounced off the target.

"You need to relax and don't drop your arm until the arrow hits the target." Brady moved beside her, putting his hands gently on her hips. "Turn this way a tiny bit." He picked up a new arrow and handed it to her. "Get ready to shoot it."

She did as he said even though his close proximity was making her heart race. He reached around her to pull her right arm back a little more and pressed against her back as he reached around with his left hand to help her aim the arrowhead higher.

"Take a deep breath in," he said with his lips by her ear. He smelled citrusy, clean, and a bit tangy. She did her best to calm her body even though her skin was tingling. "Pull back and when you let go, keep your arms right here. Don't drop them until you see that arrow go into the target."

Alexa pulled back and inhaled, exhaling as she released the arrow. Brady didn't let go. He kept her arms in the same position they were in before the arrow was launched. It hit dead center on the target. Elated, she dropped the bow, spun around, and wrapped her arms around his neck. He squeezed her tight, lifting her off the ground for a second.

"You are going to get me in trouble, but I don't care. That was awesome," he said as he hugged her even tighter.

Caught off guard, she loosened her hold on him and pulled back enough to see his face. "Why would you get in trouble?"

"Don't worry about it." He let her go, but that dimpled smile she loved had returned. "I'm so proud of you."

"I have to do it again, by myself, for it to really count."

He motioned for her to go ahead while he stepped back to stand with the rest of her group. Alexa nocked the arrow and drew it back. She remembered what Brady had said. She inhaled and took her aim. Exhaling, she released the arrow and stayed still until it hit the target. It wasn't a bull's-eye but it was right on the line.

James and Cate cheered.

Kayleigh shouted, "So close!"

Brady was still grinning from ear to ear. He held up a hand for a high five. There was a tug in her chest; she would have preferred another hug.

"You've got it. My work here is done." As he said it, Quinn appeared and called his name. There was another man standing with him. Brady's face fell. "Uh-oh."

Alexa watched as he made his way over to his brother. She hoped there wasn't a problem. The last thing the Seasonses needed was for there to be a problem that would make them more susceptible to the plans Jordan was now making without her help.

"Told ya," Kayleigh said, coming up behind her. "You guys are too cute."

"We are not *cute*."

"I didn't see him hug anyone else after he helped them get a bull's-eye."

"Maybe I'm the only one who hit the bull's-eye with his help. Ever think of that?" Alexa challenged.

Kayleigh rolled her eyes. "You should have seen your faces. You're literally living my summer-romance dream. Don't ruin it for me by saying it's not real."

"Kayleigh, leave the poor woman alone," Cate said. "Sorry. Kids these days have no filter. They think everyone wants to hear their opinion on every subject, even the ones that have nothing to do with them."

Alexa handed her bow to James and stood

next to Cate. "Brady is a friendly guy. He's nice to everyone. Right?"

Cate pressed her lips together and kept looking straight ahead.

"He is nice to everybody," Alexa said, waiting for her to agree.

Cate scratched the back of her neck. "Honestly? You are kind of living my summer-romance fantasy, too. I'd be sad if it wasn't real."

A summer romance? Was that what was happening here? For real? For a moment Alexa let herself remember how it felt when he was showing her how to hold the bow. How it felt to be in his embrace. The way he held her stare a little longer than normal. The laughs. The butterflies. The postcard.

She could call it friendship all she wanted, but Alexa was pretty sure she was living her own fantasy summer romance.

CHAPTER TWELVE

QUINN'S SCOWL DIDN'T encourage Brady to move very fast in his direction. He once again looked angry, a popular emotion for his older brother lately. He had Andrew with him, one of the new kids they'd hired for the summer season. There was no way he had seen Brady giving in to the temptation to hold Alexa in his arms, so that couldn't be why he was mad.

Last night, he had been suspicious of what Brady had been doing upstairs. The only things upstairs were guest rooms. Luckily for Brady and unfortunately for the inn, there had been a call about an electrical outage, and Quinn was too flustered to get into it with him at the time. He had needed to go check on the problem immediately.

Brady wondered if he was going to confront him about it now.

"What's up?"

"Can I have Andrew cover for you, so you

can cover the front desk while I go help Wade with a ceiling leak in the Four Seasons Room?"

"There's water leaking from the ceiling in the Four Seasons Room?"

Quinn's scowl darkened. "Isn't that what I just said? Can you cover for me?"

The Four Seasons Room was the small banquet room where they hosted parties, wedding receptions, and such. A leak in there could lead to having to cancel some of the events Brady knew had been booked for later that summer. This was the worst time for it to need renovations.

"I can cover the front desk if that's what you need me to do."

"That's what I need you to do," Quinn replied sharply before stalking off in the direction of the Four Seasons Room.

Brady let out a deep breath. "They're almost done. Archery is over in fifteen minutes. All you need to do is walk around behind everyone and make sure no one needs help and is following the rules."

Andrew rubbed his palms together nervously. "What are the rules?"

There was no time to go over all the rules. "Just make sure that no one is shooting arrows at anything other than the targets and that no one tries to retrieve their arrows before everyone is done shooting."

Nora was covering the front desk when Brady got to the lobby. "I'm here to relieve you, so you can get back to your job of standing over there." He pointed to the desk a few feet away. Nora could have easily covered the front desk alone. Quinn was always so extra.

"He likes to have two people up here at all times. You know him. He doesn't want any guest to have to wait longer than a couple of minutes. Did he tell you what's happening in the Four Seasons Room?"

"Why would the ceiling be leaking? There's nothing above that room and there hasn't been any rain if it's a roof issue."

"Wade thinks it might be the air-conditioning units that are on the roof above it. He thinks they could be leaking, maybe have been leaking for a while and the water is finally making itself known. Just what we need—an HVAC issue, water damage, and electrical problems. Dad's going to have a heart attack when he hears about this."

She wasn't kidding. Brady had heard enough of Quinn and Dad's conversations to know that the inn could not afford any big renovations right now. He wished he could do more to help than cover the front desk. Maybe he could pick Alexa's brain later tonight.

Alexa. What he wouldn't give to convince her to extend her vacation. He'd take one more week, but he'd also be a big fan of indefinitely. Sunday was creeping up on him faster than he liked. It was going to be hard to say goodbye.

A guest needing more towels interrupted his wallowing. After securing a towel delivery to Room 224, he helped a family who had lost their second key card and wanted the room recarded so whoever found it couldn't break into their room. When he finished that, he looked up to find Alexa's gorgeous green eyes looking back at him.

"Archery is finished already?"

"All done. I didn't get any more bull's-eyes, but all my arrows hit the target and stayed put thanks to your guidance." She had on a purple shirt and white shorts today. He could tell why purple was her favorite color. She looked stunning in it.

"That was all you and your need to succeed. I knew you'd figure it out. Is there anything else I can help you with, or are you just stopping by to tell me once again that I am the greatest activities director of all time?"

She laughed like she always did when he

amused her. "Your modesty is maybe my favorite character trait of yours."

"It is definitely one of my best."

They both moved closer, practically pressed against the counter separating them. "I wanted to ask about Wickets and Wine. You mentioned that you might join the event. I wanted to be sure that you meant it as in you would possibly be my buddy for it. I've had buddy anxiety ever since you told me about the—" she nodded her head in Nora's direction "—matchmaking."

"Like I told you, there is no more matchmaking for you. She has given up on matchmaking."

"That makes me very happy. Now, about being my buddy. You were kind of distant during archery until the end there. Just want to make sure everything is okay."

Brady glanced over at his sister, who was showing a guest a list of excursions and was not paying attention to what was happening at his desk. "I was trying to be professional and I knew that the second I got close to you all that was going to go—" he flicked his fingers "—*poof*. I have a really hard time controlling my need to touch you."

Her eyes flared. "Is that right?" He nodded. "Can I tell you a secret?" He nodded again. "It makes me happy that you feel that way. And I've been trying to think of ways to do more things that make me happy since our conversation last night."

"And what have you come up with so far?"

"Your mother's pastries in the morning."

"Those have been making me happy for almost thirty-three years."

She smiled crookedly at him. "Tennis."

"I need to learn."

"And then there's the big one."

"I'm all ears." He rested his elbows on the counter and leaned closer to her.

"You. Being with you. Talking to you. Eating with you. Working with you. Playing with you. Pretty much anything that involves *you*."

That was exactly where he hoped she was going with this. Heat radiated through his chest and a sense of contentment came over him like he had never experienced before. If they weren't in the lobby of the inn, he would have held her face and kissed those perfectly pink lips. Closing his eyes to kiss her was the only reason he would ever want to not be looking at her when they were together.

"We're going to need to explore that a little more after Wickets and Wine."

"I'm all for it," she replied before biting down on her bottom lip.

"Hi, Ms. Fox," Nora said, sliding over to the

check-in desk. "How was archery? Did you unleash your inner Katniss Everdeen?"

Both Brady and Alexa straightened. It was easy to forget they weren't the only two people in the world.

"It was fun. I was just thanking your brother for showing me how to do it correctly so the arrow didn't ricochet back into the grass. I was also wondering if I could sign up to do paddleboarding again? I think I want to try one more time to stand on it as I paddle around the lake."

Brady perked up. "Really? That's awesome. We let guests rent them for a few hours any day. I'm sure you don't need the tour from me again."

"I—I—" she stammered. "I wasn't sure how it worked. I don't think I want to go out alone."

"You wouldn't have to go out alone. I'd make sure you have a buddy." Brady resisted giving her a wink in front of Nora. He would make sure that the only person Alexa buddied up with from now on was him.

"That would be great. Thanks."

Nora stared an extra-long second at Brady before turning her attention back to Alexa. "I am so glad you've found something you enjoy. Is there anything else you'd like me to add to your schedule of activities?"

"Nothing else for now. I think I need a couple less-busy days. All these activities are making the days fly by too quickly. I'm not ready to leave yet!"

Wasn't that the truth? Brady would do anything to stop time for a bit.

"Totally understand," Nora empathized. "That time-is-relative thing is no joke. Why don't I look at what I have planned for you over the next couple of days and pare it down a bit? That will give you some more downtime."

"Thanks," Alexa said, tapping the counter with her fingers. "I'll let you two get back to work. The customer service at the Seasons Inn is exceptional. I plan to put that in my review."

"We aim to please," Nora replied.

Alexa's eyes flickered his way before she disappeared down the hall to the elevators.

"What was that?" Nora said, nudging Brady with her elbow.

"What was what?" Playing dumb was his best move.

"I think she was flirting with you."

"Ms. Fox?"

"Stop. I know you know what I'm talking about. You also know how dad feels about fraternizing with the guests."

"If Ms. Fox was flirting with me it's because someone has done nothing but sign her up for activities hosted by yours truly. You keep throwing me in her path. No one can resist this." He patted his chest. "Not with constant exposure. Good thing she asked for some downtime. You better go look at what you planned." An older couple shuffled up to the counter. They could not have shown up at a better time. "I need to help these next guests."

"I'm only looking out for you, Brady."

"And I appreciate it," he said before turning his attention to the guests.

Brady knew the rules. He knew that this was temporary. He understood that there could be some lectures in his future, but none of that mattered because he made Alexa happy. He was going to make sure he kept doing that.

Quinn returned to the lobby almost two hours after he had asked Brady to cover the front desk. Brady's big brother didn't have to say a word for him and Nora to know that it was bad news.

"Did you get Dad involved?" Nora asked.

"Dad is handling it. He told me to come back here and get out of everyone's way."

Brady pressed his lips together tightly so he didn't let out a laugh. It would not be welcomed by crabby Quinn. Brady could imagine exactly how annoying he had probably been while their dad and Wade were trying to problem-solve. All Quinn ever did was focus on the negative. It was like he lived under a dark cloud all the time and had a way of blocking others' sunshine when he was too close.

"Are we going to be able to use that room for the wedding reception on Saturday?" Nora asked.

Quinn shook his head. "I doubt it. But you know Dad, he thinks the show can go on no matter what. He acts like a miracle is going to happen and all the problems are going to disappear. He doesn't understand that's not reality. We have a lot of issues that need to be taken care of or people are going to stop staying here. Heck, we're going to have to stop allowing people to stay here soon."

He made it seem like they were headed for total disaster. There was no way that was true. Their dad would figure out what to do. He always did. Brady would ask Alexa what she thought when they talked later tonight.

No one but Brady and his mom came home for dinner that night. She was unsurprisingly more optimistic than Quinn but seemed to be a tad more concerned than normal. Brady tried not to read into it too much. He didn't want to let all this inn business distract him from the night he was about to have with Alexa. She was only there for three more full days. The inn's problems were still going to be there on Sunday when she left. That was when Brady would dive deeper into what was going on.

By six, he had changed into white golf shorts and a white Seasons Inn polo. He wanted to blend in, but also be able to say he was there to help monitor the event as a staff member. He knew Ivy wouldn't really care. He crashed events all the time if they were fun.

Wickets and Wine was being held on the croquet lawn. They had a little wine cart set up with glasses and various bottles in ice buckets. One of the restaurant bartenders was stationed there under a shade umbrella. Brady didn't see Alexa, so he went over to get a glass of wine and find Ivy.

Ivy found him. "Are you here to help or to be the life of the party?"

"I'm always the life of the party even when I'm helping."

"Very true. But is it one of those things or both tonight?"

"I'm here to have fun, but if you need to ruin my night, I am happy to help."

"I will do no such thing. Please, have all the fun. Then other people will realize that they, too, can have fun and this will be another successful event run by *moi*." She pressed a hand over her heart.

Ivy always ran successful events. Tonight

would be no different, Brady or no Brady. He watched as people began to gather and some started a game. His eyes drifted to the doors he assumed Alexa would come through.

"Looking for someone specific?" Suddenly, there she was, standing beside him.

Brady jumped. "Where did you come from?"

Her giggle mended every wound he had ever had. "I was taking a walk down by the lake after dinner. I didn't mean to startle you, but I have to admit I enjoyed it." She imitated his jump.

"Oh, that was funny, was it?" She nodded. Brady loved her playfulness. "I guess I will be showing no mercy on the croquet court. You, Ms. Fox, are about to lose badly."

"I will have you know that my grandparents used to have a croquet set at their house and my brother and I used to play every time we visited as kids."

"I live on a property that has a full croquet lawn. This croquet lawn, to be exact." He pointed at it for effect.

"I guess we'll see who hates losing more," she replied, unfazed by his obvious advantage. She stepped around him and asked for a glass of white wine. "Where do we get our mallets and balls?"

"Follow me." Brady led the way to the equipment beside one of the courts. There were no purple croquet balls, so Alexa chose blue. Brady picked the green one because it was his new favorite color. Alexa did practice swings with three different mallets before choosing one to use.

"That one's the winning mallet?" he asked.

She rested it on her shoulder as she walked toward the starting stake. "Yep."

Ivy had set up little tables to set the wineglasses on as people moved through the game. Brady put his wineglass next to Alexa's and followed her onto the lawn.

"Was I supposed to wear white?" she asked, surveying the court and the other guests, who had already begun playing. Several of them were dressed like Brady. Some had on white shirts or white pants. Alexa was wearing a jade-colored dress, making her stand out a bit.

"Croquet is like tennis. You're supposed to wear white, but it's not required here at the Seasons Inn. We understand that not everyone thinks to pack head-to-toe white when they're on vacation."

"Well, now I know for next time. Who goes first?"

The colors on the stake determined who went first and that was Brady with green. He hit it through the first wicket and the second wicket with no problem. The third wicket was diagonal from the last one and farther away. He hit it close enough that when it was his turn again, he'd be able to hit it through.

Alexa hit her ball through the first two wickets on one hit. She didn't say anything, but she smiled smugly as she walked to her ball. Her second shot hit Brady's ball with a cracking sound.

"Come on," Brady said to the sky, tipping his head back. Hitting another player's ball meant two bonus hits. She continued to smirk as she made her way over to their side-by-side balls. She put her foot on her ball and swung her mallet, hitting it on the side opposite of the one touching his ball. The physics of it all sent his ball rolling away from the wicket and making it almost impossible for him to get through it in one shot when it was his turn. Brady went to get his wineglass. Something told him it wasn't going to be his turn anytime soon.

Alexa had not been kidding about being good at croquet. She hit her second bonus shot through the third wicket, meaning it was still her turn. Eventually, Brady got to play again, but all in all, this was Alexa's game and she won it easily.

When she struck the final stake, she spun around to face him with her hands in the air and the biggest grin on her face. Brady had refilled their wineglasses and handed Alexa hers so they could toast to her win.

"To the true champion of croquet. I didn't stand a chance, apparently."

"I tried to warn you." She tapped her glass against his and took a sip, keeping her eyes locked on his.

Maybe it was her dress, maybe it was the fact that the sun was setting, but her eyes were like sparkling jewels tonight. "Can I take you somewhere?"

Without hesitating, she said, "Sure."

He took her mallet and ball and had her hold his wine for him. He turned in the equipment and hustled back to where she waited. He took his glass back, and her hand, twining their fingers together. Then he led her down the path that took them to the east side of the beach. There was a large sugar maple at the edge of the property. Hanging from one of the larger branches was a two-person swing that offered one of the best views of the sunset over the mountains.

"This is quite the spot," she said, taking a seat.

Brady settled in next to her. "This was my idea. I know this won't surprise you, but I did not write a plan or get my dad's permission to install it. I went into town and bought everything I needed for it and had Wade help me make sure it was safe."

"How rebellious of you."

"It was my gift to my mom on Mother's Day about five years ago. With the way we're situated on the south end of the lake and with all the shade trees on the property, she always felt like we were lacking a good viewing area for people to watch the sunset. I knew that meant *she* lacked a good spot to watch the sunset, so when I found this tree after we had a big storm and we had to clean up a fallen tree that used to stand right down there, blocking this view, I knew I had found the perfect spot for a swing and the sunset."

Alexa tucked some hair behind her ear. "That is the sweetest thing. You're a good son."

"She's a good mom."

"Stop, I can't take it." She took a sip of her wine and looked out over the water. They sat together in silence, taking in the view. Alexa crossed her legs at her ankles and let her shoulder lean against his.

"Since I put the swing in, we've had about ten marriage proposals take place here. My sister loves to tell couples about it."

"I can see why it would be popular for something like that." Alexa kept her gaze fixed on the view in front of them.

The sun had begun to drop behind the mountains, an orange half circle shooting its rays down the mountainside. It cast a golden glow over the lake, so different from the morning, when the lake looked like it was sparkling with little white lights.

The setting sun gave Alexa's skin a golden sheen as well. She was a green-and-gold goddess. Her hair fluttered in the wind and tickled his arm. Her lips curved up as the sun sank farther down. Brady rested his arm along the back of the swing behind her.

"Beautiful," he sighed.

"It really is," she replied, unaware that he had been talking about her, not the sunset. She glanced his way and caught him staring.

"You're not even looking," she said with a nervous giggle.

"I can see the sunset anytime I want. You're only here until Sunday." It was then he knew with their time so short, it was now or never. He reached up and cupped her cheek. She didn't pull away, but she let out a soft gasp. Her skin was so soft. He wondered if her lips felt the same. Brady leaned in and waited for her to tell him to stop. She didn't say anything, and leaned in as well, and when their lips touched, it was pure magic.

CHAPTER THIRTEEN

BRADY HAD KISSED HER. Alexa had to tell someone. It wasn't going to be real until she told someone. She had gone back to her room after they had spent several minutes making out on the tree swing. Neither of them had known what to say when they stopped. They had just crossed a big line.

So what did she do? Alexa immediately reminded him that they were supposed to work on his proposal tonight. Why did she always default to work? Brady had seemed confused for a second, but agreed that they should get started if they wanted to be done by a reasonable hour. He was now at his house, getting the homework notes he had written on real paper this time. They had agreed to meet in an hour. She had one hour to call Melody and freak out.

"Hey, there. I didn't expect to hear from you. Is everything okay?" Melody asked when she answered the phone.

"I kissed Brady," Alexa blurted. Talk about

acting like a teenager. She couldn't even spit out a proper greeting.

"What? Hold on, don't answer that." Melody's voice was muffled as she spoke to her husband. "Honey, can you make sure the kids start getting ready for bed in fifteen minutes? I really need to take this call in the other room. No one bother me."

Alexa laughed. She knew Melody would be excited for her. She needed someone to be excited for her. It had been a year of everyone feeling sad for her. It was nice to talk about something happy.

"Okay, I'm ready to hear all about this kiss." Alexa could hear a door close.

"I don't know what I'm doing, Mel."

"You're having the greatest vacation of all time, that's what you're doing."

"But I'm leaving on Sunday. Why would I kiss someone when I know I'm leaving in a few days?"

"Because that's what single people do. They make out with random guys and enjoy the moment. It doesn't have to mean you two are going to get married."

Alexa had never been a make-out-with-random-guys kind of girl. This also did not feel like making out with someone random. Brady was not random. He was a real person. Someone she had gotten to know. Someone she liked. A lot.

"It feels a bit more serious than a random make-out," she said.

"Lex, the guy is gorgeous, single, and works at a place where new people come to stay every week or so. He's probably made out with tons of women. Trust me, he has done this before many times."

Alexa wasn't sure whom she was more offended on behalf of, herself or Brady. He was not some playboy who sought out lonely women and made out with them every week. She did not for a second believe that about him.

"Well, to be honest, that kind of hurts my feelings and is taking away from the absolute high I was on a minute ago. How can you think that I'm just another sad, single lady who some lothario has tricked into thinking she's special?"

"That's not what I meant!" Melody said, backpedaling. "I think you are special—really special. I was there. I saw Brady. I don't think he hits on everyone. I think you have to be special for him to pick you."

"So he hits on lots of women, but you have to be special for him to pick you? Is that what you're saying?" She was quickly regretting making this phone call.

"No. I'm trying to make you feel better about

leaving. I'm trying to tell you that it's okay to do something spontaneous and fun without having to worry about what it means. It just means he wanted to kiss you and so he did."

Alexa tried to see it the way she was now spinning it. There was no reason she couldn't kiss a cute guy that she wasn't going to start dating. She didn't have to have some long-term plan to have fun with someone for a couple of days.

"What if it makes me sad to leave? I am trying so hard not to make this into something it's not, but he is really amazing. He is the nicest guy I have ever met. He's funny. He's adventurous. He's patient. Oh, my gosh, Mel, he is so patient. He has never once made me feel bad about needing extra help with something or just being bad at it. He's always checking in, asking me if I'm okay. And not just me. He does that with everyone. He's so nice to everyone here. And don't get me started on what kind of son he is. Mel, he's literally the sweetest son on the planet. His mom raised a good man."

"Oh, no."

"What do you mean 'oh, no'?"

"Did you fall in love with Brady, the activities director?"

That was a wild accusation. Alexa had been at the Seasons Inn for a full five days. No one fell in love in five days. Except for all those people who claimed to fall in love at first sight—maybe they fell in love in less than five days. It wasn't an issue of *if*, but of *can't*.

"I can't fall in love with Brady. There's no way we could work. He loves working at the inn. His family is here. He would never move to New York for someone like me."

"Someone like you? Who's trying to hurt your feelings now? You are not just anyone. You are a great catch for any guy."

"Ha, tell that to Brett."

"Brett wanted something different than he thought he wanted when he married you. He didn't try to grow with you, he tried to stop you from growing, tried to get you to change so you'd be what he wanted instead of asking what you wanted."

Alexa let out a flustered breath. That was true. Brett had wanted to navigate the relationship himself and got mad when she didn't follow his lead every single time. He had no patience for her. He wanted her to want what he wanted when he wanted it. Period.

Brady wasn't like that. He cared about her being happy. He'd already proven that. He would never ask her to give up something that made her happy—but also wasn't going to sacrifice his own happiness for hers.

"I think that even if he thinks I am the woman

of his dreams, he would still let me go, because he knows that he wouldn't be happy in New York."

"Are you even happy in New York anymore?" Melody's question struck a chord. Alexa hadn't been happy for so long.

"My job is in New York. I can't quit my job and run away from New York because I feel sad after my divorce."

"True. Can we go back to just being giddy about this kiss?"

The conversation had taken a turn. "It was a pretty phenomenal kiss. He probably has kissed a lot of people because he's really good at it."

When he had cupped her cheek, she'd melted into a puddle of goo at his feet. Her heart had been beating so hard she'd been afraid it was going to malfunction from overuse. He had been so gentle and there'd been nothing remotely lewd about it. He had been a total gentleman. And when she got up to leave, he hadn't pouted or acted as if she had led him on; he had seemed just as flustered—and happy—as she was.

"Where were you when this happened? You'd think he'd need to be careful since he works there."

"We were down by the lake. There's this old tree with a swing that has the best view of the sunset. It was the perfect moment in the perfect spot."

"Oh, man. That's one heck of a first kiss. He might make it really hard to date guys back in New York."

That was for sure. How could anyone compare to Brady? "Should I say anything to him? How do I act now that we've kissed? I have three more full days here. Sunday is right around the corner."

Melody let out a long breath. "Part of me wants to tell you to play it off. Act like nothing happened and see what he does and says. The other part of me wants to tell you to enjoy every second you have left there. Take what you can get, Lex, because you're going to be back in New York in no time and, knowing you, that means full steam ahead with work. You might not kiss a guy again until your next vacation."

That was sadly the truth. Alexa had no time for dating. She wasn't sure she even wanted to date. Before meeting Brady, she really didn't think she'd find a decent enough guy to make her want to jump into another relationship after Brett. She kind of felt like relationships weren't all they were made out to be. Kissing Brady, however, made her realize that falling for someone could actually be a million times better than what she remembered it being like with Brett.

"I think I'll see how he acts around me and go from there."

"That's probably the best plan. I hope if nothing else, you realize that you are a lovable person. You deserve good things. You shouldn't be afraid to have some fun. And hot guys are not unattainable, my friend."

Alexa laughed at that last point. When Melody and Alexa were in high school, they used to discuss the fact that the really hot guys were out of their league. They had accepted their fate that they were going to have to settle for a "generally attractive" guy, because they were both in that same category. You couldn't be a six and think you were going to date a ten. That wasn't the way the world worked. Alexa wasn't sure if the rules had changed as she got older, or if she was actually higher than a six, because Brady was definitely a solid ten.

Alexa hung up with her friend, promising to keep her posted. She now had three people in this world rooting for her summer romance. She wondered what Cate and Kayleigh would say about the romantic turn things had taken. Not that she would be discussing it with them. She knew that Brady had to be careful. She was a guest at his family's inn. Another reason this fantasy relationship could not turn into reality.

Brady knocked on her door exactly one hour

from when he told her he was going to meet her up there. He had his notebook in hand and didn't mention anything about the kiss.

"You did your homework?"

"To the best of my ability, yes." He handed her the notebook. "I asked my dad a few questions and I called a few places. I think I got the answers you were looking for."

"Awesome. I also did some digging earlier today." She opened her laptop and patted the seat next to her on the couch. She knew he liked to move around when they worked, but she needed him to see her screen.

Brady sat down but his left leg started bouncing almost instantly. "What is all this?"

"I made a spreadsheet. Down here, I have tabs for the four different seasons, so when I'm gone and you're filling this out, you can add the information for the other seasons. Right now, we're focused on summer. I have the names of all the businesses you mentioned that might be willing to participate in some way." She went through the different bits of information. "The biggest issue for me was making sure we had the correct information about permits or permissions. From what I learned from a very nice lady named Greta at the Apple Hollow clerk's office, there are a couple of permits you would need."

"I never would have thought to look into that." Brady squinted as he read the screen.

"I'm sure someone would have thought of it, but it looks good for you if you have that in your proposal."

"I don't think I'm going to be able to present this by myself. Any chance I can hire you to do the presentation for me?"

"This is your idea. You believe in it. No one can sell it the way you can."

He sat back and crossed his legs, resting his ankle on top of his other knee. "But you explain things so much better than me. You know how to be clear and concise. I ramble," he argued.

"I will make sure you've got it down. We'll practice. I'll pretend to be your dad and give you feedback."

Brady sighed. "Yeah, my brother is never going to believe that I did all this stuff on my own."

"So what if you didn't? What's wrong with getting help so that it's the best proposal it can be?"

"I'm guessing you have never felt like the inferior sibling before."

Alexa got defensive on his behalf. She slammed her laptop shut and set it on the coffee table. "You are not the inferior sibling. You are one of the most impressive people I have ever had the privilege of knowing. Your siblings would have to be the most incredible humans on the entire planet to make you look inferior, and I have met two of your siblings and as nice as they are, they do not hold a candle to your kindness, your empathy, your—"

In the middle of her sentence, Brady shifted. He grabbed her face and kissed her. Once the shock wore off, Alexa allowed herself to experience the pure joy that came with kissing Brady Seasons. He pulled back and pressed his forehead against hers.

"I have waited a very long time for someone to see me the way you do."

That was so hard to believe. How could people not see what she saw? Brady was everything Alexa wished she could be. Balanced. He worked hard and made time to play hard, too. "There's no other way to see you."

He sat back but took hold of Alexa's hand. "I wish that was true, but I think people look at Quinn and Theo and see two people who are smart, accomplished, and have direction in their lives. They see me and think I'm just the *other* brother. The one who still acts like a kid, going kayaking and paddleboarding every day."

"You do a lot more than that. Plus, you are a smart guy. I've spent all this time with you listening to your ideas about how to bring your community together while also increasing business to the inn. When we put all those ideas together and you show your dad, he's going to let you run this whole place when he retires."

He held up a hand to stop her. "Let's not get carried away here. I don't want to run the place. I want to keep going kayaking and paddleboarding and four-wheeling—all the things I do now. I love that stuff. I have the best job. I wouldn't mind being taken a bit more seriously, though."

She loved that he knew his limits and set boundaries. Things she wasn't good at doing in her own career. He truly tried to live by his philosophy of working to live instead of living to work.

"Well, I am happy to do whatever I can to help make that a reality for you," she said.

He dipped his chin and flashed her a smile. "Thank you."

The way he looked at her made her want to kiss him again. That impulse needed to be reined in. It was time to talk about the elephant in the room.

"Can we talk about this?" She motioned between the two of them.

"I was wondering if we were going to do that."

"I'm leaving on Sunday."

"I know." His gaze fell to their hands. He still held one of hers in his.

"I think we both understand that we can't be more than this, right?"

His eyes met hers. "You don't want to give up your life in New York, move to a small town in New Hampshire, and get to know me better?" The look on his face made it clear that he wasn't serious.

"If we keep kissing like that, I might be convinced." She also wasn't serious but she couldn't deny those kisses made the thought very tempting.

He perked up and patted his pockets. "If that's all it's going to take, I need to find my lip balm."

Alexa laughed and gave him a gentle push. "Stop."

"If you want to go ahead without it, I'm happy to comply," he said, playfully closing his eyes and puckering his lips as if waiting for her to plant a kiss on them. He opened one eye and frowned. "No?"

"I need you to be serious."

His expression turned somber. "I can do that."

"What are we doing?" Maybe he could figure it out because she was baffled.

"We're attracted to each other. Obviously, I shouldn't have kissed you, but I couldn't help myself. When we were sitting on that swing… and the way you are, the things you say, the way you look… I can't resist acting on my feelings.

I can't promise you that I won't get the impulse again. I literally have a medical diagnosis that's all about my lack of impulse control."

"So your ADHD made you kiss me?"

"*You* made me kiss you. I can't deny that I like you. I know you're leaving. I wish you weren't. I know it would be absurd to ask you to try to have some kind of long-distance relationship with me. I am painfully aware that this has a very specific time limit. I also think, what's wrong with making the most of the time we have left?"

Embarrassment that she couldn't just live so freely caused her to avert her gaze. Was she a prude? She certainly wasn't savvy when it came to this kind of stuff. She hadn't dated since she was in college, which felt like a million years ago. She also didn't kiss people who she had no intention of being in a relationship with—not that if circumstances were different, she wouldn't happily start a relationship with Brady. It simply wasn't possible.

"I am not sure that I can act on feelings without consequences. I think I need the boundary that we're just friends. Friends who don't kiss." She waited for him to respond.

Brady nodded, his lips pressed together in a thin line.

"It's not that I didn't enjoy kissing you. I enjoyed it. Like I told you before, I have the most fun when I'm with you. I am just not sure my heart can handle being casual about it, though. I can't pretend that it doesn't mean anything. Come Sunday, I won't be able to drive away like those feelings didn't matter, because if these feelings get any bigger than they are..." She paused, trying to think of the right words to say without making him think she was some overly clingy romantic who thought she was in love. Deep down, though, she knew being close to Brady could be life-changing. There was no doubt about that. "I don't know. I think if they got bigger, it would make leaving hurt more."

"That makes total sense. No more kissing. I don't know that my heart would like me messing around with it like that, either. We're friends. We enjoy each other's company and we're going to do that for the next several days. And when you leave, I'm going to give you a very long goodbye hug, and I am going to wish you well and remind you that you are always welcome back at the Seasons Inn anytime the spirit moves you in this direction."

Alexa fidgeted with her bracelet. It was a relief that he could see it her way. It also meant a lot that he hoped she'd be back someday. "I mean, I probably need to come back for one of your Seasons at the Lake days. I can't help you sell it to your dad and then not see it come to fruition."

"That is true." His smile was back. "I do think it will be necessary for you to be here for that."

She reached for her laptop. "That means we need to get this proposal put together. Kissing was a lovely distraction, but we can't afford any more of those."

Brady emphasized his agreement with a strong nod. "Let's stay on task. I would like to present the idea to my dad while you're here so we can celebrate or you can tell me what I did wrong."

He wasn't going to do anything wrong. Brady's idea was solid. "Let's look at the notes you brought."

He glanced around. "Where did I put those? I have a tendency to lose things like notes and homework. Did I mention that when you told me there would be homework?"

"You gave it to me." Alexa found it had slipped off the arm of the couch, perhaps during that mind-blowing kiss he'd surprised her with earlier. What a kiss it had been. Maybe Melody was right and she should just go for it because who knew when she would ever get kissed like this again.

Stay on task.

Brady wasn't the only one who would need

to be reminded. She paged through his notes as his phone chimed with a text.

"Oh, man."

"What's going on?" Alexa asked, sucked right off task again by his tone.

"Sounds like we're going to have to move a wedding reception because the air conditioners on the roof above the Four Seasons Room are causing water to drip from the ceiling. And since it's the summer and we cannot turn off the AC to stop the condensation, there's no way to stop that water from dripping and no one wants water dripping from the ceiling at their wedding reception."

Oh, man was right. The inn was going to be in a very vulnerable position if they were going to have to upgrade their electrical system and fix air conditioners and a leaky roof. Brady's dad was going to have to find money for all that stuff. Money, Jordan had made clear, that he didn't have. There had to be something, somewhere.

"What kind of emergency fund does your dad usually keep? He must have money put aside for these kinds of things."

Brady inhaled and made a face like he wasn't sure that was fact. "I'm not really on top of all the financial stuff, but Quinn is and he's in full meltdown mode. He's texting me and Nora that we need to consider how we, personally, can help. He'd like us to take a good look at our own finances. I'm not sure I understand what he wants me to do—let the HVAC guy charge my credit card when he comes to fix the air conditioners?"

Alexa felt like a shark swimming in the water with wounded prey. If it wasn't for her feelings for Brady, she'd be scheduling a meeting with his dad before she left. She would be presenting this place to Roger over the phone without Jordan's help, and Roger would jump on it because it was easy money.

His text notification rang out again. "Oh, I see. He wants us to chip in to cover the property taxes that are due on the first of next month. There's no way our dad will let us do that. What are the chances we even have enough to cover that?"

Alexa's chest ached. She had already done that research before she got there. She knew they paid almost two hundred thousand dollars a year in property taxes alone. New Hampshire also required businesses to pay a business profits tax. They were also behind in payments according to the public site she had visited.

"The fact that this property has stayed in your family's name for as long as it has without having to take on some kind of investor is really impressive. Not many places like this can manage that."

Brady cocked his head. "How do you know that?"

She froze. How could she explain why she had any information about the ownership of the inn? "You don't have a hidden private-equity firm that can get you out of all this trouble, do you?" she asked, trying to play it off as if she simply assumed it.

"I don't even know what a private-equity firm is so I don't think we have one of those. My great-grandfather built the first version of the Seasons Inn. He used his profits to buy up more and more of the land around it, so he could make it the grandest place in all of New Hampshire. My dad always says there's no way Great-grandpa could have imagined how amazing it would become. It's always been a source of pride that it's a family-owned business."

"You don't have a rich uncle somewhere who might want to keep the family business in the family?"

"No rich uncles. Just a rich brother."

"Quinn's rich?" It was Alexa's turn to be confused.

"No, Theo. He's a professional hockey player. The guy makes more money than all of us combined."

Alexa stared at him, her eyes trying to convey the obvious question.

"Oh, no. My dad's pride would never let Theo bail him out. On top of that, Theo doesn't want anything to do with the inn. He barely wants anything to do with the family. That's what happens when you're a hotshot hockey star who couldn't get out of this small town fast enough."

The famous hockey-playing brother in Boston. Alexa hadn't made that connection. Theo might not have anything to do with the inn, but Jordan didn't need to know that. There was a chance she could protect the Seasons Inn after all.

CHAPTER FOURTEEN

NOT KISSING ALEXA should have been easy. Brady had spent thirty-three years not doing it. Why was it all he thought about now? It had to be because he had agreed not to do it. That was how his brain liked to torture him.

He had agreed to take her paddleboarding again on Friday. This time, she was determined to stand. Unfortunately, her body had other plans. She got to her feet and as soon as she took that second hand off the board, she rocked to the side and fell into the lake.

She came up for air and smacked the water with her hand. "I hate this. Why can't I do it?"

Brady paddled closer. "I feel like it's just a mental block at this point. You want it too bad."

"I want to not keep falling in the water, that's what I want." Cute, flustered Alexa was in full force.

"Let's move closer to shore, where I can stand in the water and help balance the board."

"That's cheating," she said, pulling herself

back up on her board. Her hair was wet and matted to her head. Rivulets of water ran down her face. She wiped her eyes as she fumed.

"It's not cheating. It's helping you get the feel for it. Once you realize how to find your center of gravity, you're going to be fine and I won't have to hold anything."

"Fine," she huffed as she paddled on her knees back to shore.

Brady jumped off his board once the water was about waist-deep. "I'm going to hold things steady. I want you to do exactly what you've been doing. Start on your knees. Put one foot by your hand, lift up, put your other foot where the other hand was and you'll be standing. Remember to look forward, not down. Pick a spot out there before we start."

"You are going to make a great dad someday," she said, catching him off guard. "You have so much patience. I envy that."

Brady didn't think he was ready for kids. In some ways, he felt like he was still a kid. It was nice to hear that someone saw that potential in him, though. "If you keep talking to me like that I'm going to make you fall in the water so I can kiss you again," he teased.

"Friends only, buddy," she said, wagging a finger at him. "You better keep me on this board at all times."

He had agreed to the friends-only thing, but he knew she was kidding herself if she didn't want him to break their rule at least one more time. For now, he would be good. *Friends.* Friends helped friends stand on a paddleboard.

She refocused on the task. "I'm going to look at that guy in the fishing boat straight ahead who hasn't moved in a while."

"Perfect, let's go. You've got this. Stand up."

She went through the motions and when she lifted up after planting that first foot, he needed to put some extra muscle into holding the board still because she was rocking it.

"I've got you. Put the other foot where your hand is," he directed her.

Alexa did as she was told and moved her foot into place. She kept her head up and her eyes glued to the fishing boat. Brady kept the board still and Alexa found her balance.

"I'm doing it!"

"You are. Now, don't look down, but start using your paddle to move forward. Don't look away from that boat. Imagine paddling all the way to that guy and asking him if he's caught anything yet."

Alexa started paddling and didn't even notice Brady wasn't holding her board steady anymore until he caught up to her and was paddling beside her.

"Good job," he said, causing her to turn her head in his direction and lose sight of the fishing boat. She started to wobble. "Look straight, look straight!"

She recovered and nervous laughter bubbled out of her. "Oh, my gosh, I can't believe I didn't fall in."

"I should have warned you that I was coming up next to you. Keep paddling. The momentum helps. The more you have, the more stable you are."

Just like he knew she would, Alexa had figured out how to stay upright on her board. She was able to make turns and followed him as they did a loop around the lake. The comfortable feeling that he had when he was around her had a bittersweet edge to it. Spending time with her was so easy, yet he could hear that ticking clock in his head. She wasn't going to be here next week to go paddleboarding with or to see how she fared at kayaking.

Brady pushed down the sad feelings because Alexa was beaming with pride when they got back to shore in front of the Seasons Inn. "That was way more fun on my feet. Thank you for taking me out and not leaving me pouting in the water."

"Hey, it's frustrating when things don't go the

way we want them to. Cut yourself some slack for being a normal human with feelings."

She lifted her board out of the water. "You always have the best perspective."

"Hey, I knew you'd get it. You're a very determined person."

"We forgot to make it a race. Should we go back out and see who can get to the cove first?"

Even though he was always up for some friendly competition, there was somewhere else he wanted to take her today. "If we go back to race, we'll be out there all day because you won't give up until you win. You're very competitive and I would never let you win without truly earning it."

"You think it would take me all day to beat you?" She had her hand on her hip. "Or you think the only way it would happen quickly is if you *let* me win? I may have struggled to get on my feet, but now that I've done it, there's no telling what I'll be able to do out there."

"Are you like this in all aspects of your life?" he asked with a chuckle. He stopped at the picnic table on the beach and set his board on top. "I picture you in a boardroom staring down guys twice your age, badgering them until they give you what you want."

"That's not what I do."

"Come to think of it, I don't even know what

you do for a living. You talked about getting a degree in accounting and you sure knew a lot about taxes last night. Are you some kind of super accountant who fights taxes with one hand tied behind your back?" He jokingly did some shadowboxing with one arm.

She didn't laugh like he'd expected her to. She came up behind him, placing her board on the ground.

"I am not an accountant anymore. I do consulting mostly. It's boring stuff. I don't think your attention span could appreciate me saying any more than that."

"Oh, come on. Give me a little more credit than that. I might find what you do extremely interesting if I can understand any of the business terms that you use to explain it. Go on, what exactly do you do at that fancy job of yours in New York?"

Alexa remained unamused. She snatched one of the beach towels they had left on the picnic table bench for when they returned. "I don't want to talk about work when I'm on vacation. Can we drop it?"

It seemed to pain her more than anything, so he had no issue with changing the subject. "Absolutely."

He put the boards back in the storage shed while Alexa dried off and put on her swim cover-up. She sat down at the picnic table and gazed out over the lake. It was like one of Quinn's dark clouds had hovered over her. Maybe she was thinking about the same things Brady was. Maybe the timer was counting down in her mind as well.

"I don't have to lead an activity until later this afternoon," he said, taking a seat across from her. "I was sort of hoping I could take you somewhere for lunch, so I can show you one more really cool thing about Apple Hollow before you leave."

She offered him a smile that faded quickly. "You don't have to do that."

"I want to, but if you don't want to have lunch with me—"

"No, that's not it. It just feels like a date."

Brady's throat felt dry. She didn't want to date him. He had to remind himself that she couldn't date him. It might not have anything to do with want. "We'll go Dutch for lunch. We'll just be two friendly acquaintances getting lunch and doing a little bit of sightseeing."

Alexa contemplated his offer in the longest moment of silence he'd endured in recent memory. Finally, she nodded her head. "That would be nice. As long as I'm not interfering with your workday any more than I already have."

"It's all good. Why don't we get cleaned up

and meet in the lobby at noon? Wear comfortable walking shoes and some sunscreen."

She agreed to meet him there and got up to go inside. Brady headed home to take a shower and put on some dry clothes. Taking her to the summit of Maple Peak was the plan. He wanted her to see everything and the best way to do that was from up high.

Brady knew there wasn't anything he could do to convince Alexa to extend her trip, but if there was a chance something could spark her interest in making a return visit, he believed the beauty of the area was his best bet. It would be nice when she left to know there was a possibility of seeing her again.

It was a dangerous thought. He knew that, but this wasn't something that originated in his brain. This was his silly heart, and it wanted what it wanted.

After showering, Brady packed a backpack and tossed it into his car before heading back to the inn. Alexa wasn't in the lobby when he got there. Quinn wasn't at the front desk, either, which was odd. Nora was covering.

"Don't tell me Quinn actually took a lunch break."

Nora shook her head. "He's been in the office with Dad for the last hour. They've been trying to find someone to fix the ceiling in the Four

Seasons Room at least temporarily so we don't have to ask the bride and groom to move their reception outdoors. Dad thinks if we offer to put up the party tent at a discount, they'll agree. Quinn thinks we can't afford to give them a discount or lose their business. I don't think they're having much luck coming up with anyone to solve all their problems."

Brady hadn't missed the fact that no one had asked for his help in coming up with a solution. It could have been that his Dad didn't really want anyone's opinion, but Quinn gave his, anyway. It could also be that he respected Quinn's opinions over anyone else's.

"What are you up to?" she asked him, pulling him from his thoughts.

"I'm going to grab some lunch in town. I don't have anything else until I take that group out zip-lining."

"That's right." She glanced over his shoulder. "Ms. Fox looks like she's lost. I should go ask if she needs help."

Brady jumped into action. "I got it. You've got the desk to cover. I can help her out on my way out."

"Oh, thanks," Nora said, unaware that Alexa was looking for him. The matchmaker was completely clueless that she had matched Ms. Fox with someone that first day—it just wasn't Mr. Leroy.

Brady hustled over to Alexa. "Hey, my sister noticed you seemed like you needed some help. Were you trying to find a way into town for lunch?" he asked, gesturing in Nora's direction so Alexa was aware that they were being observed.

"I was." She nodded, playing along. "I wanted to see if there was a way to get into town for some lunch. Thank you for noticing."

"Perfect. Why don't you follow me out, and we'll get you a ride."

They made their escape. They had to dodge Maureen, who was pushing a luggage cart full of suitcases on the other side of the front door. Brady went back to get the door for her.

"Where are you headed, Mr. Brady?"

"I'm going into town to get some lunch. I'd bring you something back, but I have another stop after that."

Maureen pushed the cart through the door and stopped so they were face-to-face. "You are very sweet, but I brought my leftovers from last night. Meat loaf. It's my husband's favorite, but the man won't eat leftovers, so I have to chow down on meat-loaf sandwiches for the next couple of days."

"You're a saint, Mo," he said with a shake of his head. "I would make that husband of yours eat the leftovers whether he liked it or not."

She waved him off. "Trust me, he ate his fill last night. Have a good lunch with Ms. Fox."

Caught off guard, Brady stumbled over his words. "I'm… We're… She… It's not…"

Maureen just smiled and pushed the cart farther in. "Uh-huh. Have fun."

Alexa, who had been waiting for him, laughed. "You thought you were going to pull one over on Maureen?"

"Foolish. I should have known better."

They jumped into his car and headed into town. He took her to Apple Hollow Brewery and Kitchen, Brady's favorite lunch spot. They had the best burgers in the whole county as far as he was concerned. They also made their own Parmesan garlic potato chips. Their hard apple cider wasn't too bad, either.

It was a newer establishment in town but was housed in what used to be the Apple Hollow Theater back in the day. The historic building still had the original mosaic tiles on the floor by the entrance. It also boasted brick walls and high ceilings with exposed steel beams. They were seated at one of the high-top tables in the center of the dining area.

"You've been a little light on details when it comes to what we're doing after lunch," Alexa noted while they were waiting for their food to come.

"I thought I might take you to the top of Maple Peak."

"We're hiking to the top of a mountain?" Her eyes went wide.

"I have a better way to get you up there. You'll see."

"ATVs?" she asked.

Brady shook his head. "You haven't done anything like this yet."

She pondered that for a minute. "That doesn't help me because there are a million things I haven't done."

"Well, as long as I'm your activities director, I am going to make sure you do things that you've never done before. I want this vacation to blow all the other vacations you've ever taken out of the water."

"Wait, does it have to do with water? Once we make it up there, we're not going to ride down the mountain in a canoe or kayak or something, are we? Can you even go down a mountain that way?"

He nearly choked on his drink. After wiping his mouth with the back of his hand, he set his glass on the cardboard coaster in front of him.

"No, there's no canoeing down the mountain. I was thinking about doing the barrel ride down the falls but decided you had been underwater enough today."

She wadded up her cocktail napkin and threw it at him for teasing her. "I am not very knowledgeable about all the ways one would get up and down a mountain."

"You don't have to guess. You can simply wait for me to take you there."

"I could google it and then I wouldn't have to wait." She fluttered her eyelashes and pulled her phone from the cross-body bag she'd brought.

"Stop!" Brady snatched it away. "I want to see your face when we get there."

She tried to grab it back. "Fine, I won't look. Give it back."

The phone started to ring and Brady glanced at the screen. "Oh, who's Jordan?"

"Brady." Alexa doubled her efforts and wrangled the phone away. She sent the call to voice mail. Just like earlier, she went from playful to unamused very fast.

"I didn't mean to make you upset." Curiosity was coursing through his veins, though. Who was Jordan? Was Jordan a man or a woman? That wasn't her ex's name, but she seemed worried when Brady said his name. Like there was something about Jordan she did not want him to know about.

Alexa shook her head. "You didn't make me upset. Jordan is a coworker. He doesn't seem to understand what being on vacation means."

Jordan was only a guy from work. That was better than a guy friend. Not that Brady had any reason to care who Alexa was or was not friends with back in New York. There was nothing keeping her from having as many friends or dates or boyfriends as she wanted. She often talked about work consuming all her time. Did that mean she spent a lot of time with Jordan? Brady needed to stop overthinking it. He had a lot of female coworkers and he wasn't interested in dating any of them.

Alexa put her phone away and changed the subject. "After paddleboarding this morning, my brain was full of ideas for the summer Seasons at the Lake. What about a build-your-own-boat competition for kids? You could get the local hardware store to donate some building materials, the kids can put together little boats, and then you can have a race later in the day."

"I like that idea."

"And what about a boat parade with real boats? There are plenty of people with boats on the lake. You could come up with a theme every year and people could decorate their boats accordingly. The boat parade would be the way for them to show off their hard work. Maybe a local business could sponsor a competition for the boaters who capture the theme the best."

"I love all that. You came up with those today?"

"I came up with maybe six ideas," she said with a laugh. He was happy to see the sparkle back in her eyes. "It's fun to think of ways to create community and engage businesses to work together. The teamwork aspect appeals to me instead of businesses competing against each other."

"But you've found a way to build plenty of competition into the day, still."

"Right, but not between the sponsors. That's how you'll get more people to want to be involved."

"Those are great ideas. I want to add those to the proposal. Any homework I need to do before I add them?"

"You could talk to someone at the hardware store, get an idea of whether they'd be interested in contributing to something like that."

Brady knew Rodney Burke, the owner of the hardware store, pretty well. He was a few years older than Quinn and had taken over the family's store after his dad passed away a couple years ago. He made a note on his phone to give Burke Hardware a call.

Alexa, who was seated facing the entrance, leaned across the table and lowered her voice. "Two people just walked in and they are staring at us—you probably more so than me. I assume they know you. They seem to be having quite the argument about what to do."

Plenty of people in Apple Hollow knew Brady. However, he didn't think that any of them would be anxious about seeing him. Except...

"Is it a man and a woman?" he asked, not wanting to turn around.

"Yes."

"Does she have dark hair and does he have a long beard?"

"Yes." She glanced over his shoulder and quickly sat up straight in her seat. "They're coming this way."

Brady braced himself. He knew exactly who was about to ruin his lunch.

"Hey, Brady," a familiar voice said from behind him.

He shifted, turning to the left to make eye contact. His heart began pounding so hard, he could hear it in his ears. He hadn't seen her since they broke up. She looked the same but everything was different. "Hi, Sabrina. Dylan. How's it going?"

CHAPTER FIFTEEN

ALEXA QUICKLY PUT two and two together. The woman had to be Brady's ex and the guy was her new fiancé. Her heart hurt for him, knowing this unexpected encounter couldn't be easy.

"Didn't expect to see you out and about. You're usually at the inn on a day like today," his ex said, her eyes moving from Brady to Alexa and back again.

"Taking a lunch break in town today," Brady replied. His smile was so tight. Alexa wished they were sitting next to one another so she could give his hand or leg a supportive squeeze.

"I'm not sure if you heard or not—" Sabrina began.

"I heard," Brady interrupted. "I guess congratulations are in order."

"Thanks, Brady," Sabrina said, but her focus shifted to Alexa. "Are you going to introduce us to your friend?"

Brady appeared unsure of how to proceed.

Alexa decided to take the reins. She plastered on her smile and gave a little wave. "Hi, I'm Alexa."

"You aren't from around here," the bearded guy said in somewhat of an accusatory tone.

"I am not." She stopped herself from adding anything snarky about the obviousness of his observation. "I'm a business consultant from out of town."

"Business consultant?" Sabrina barked a laugh. "Oh, honey, you're talking to the wrong Seasons brother. You should be talking to Quinn. He's the one who handles all the business for the inn."

"Oh, I am definitely meeting with the right person. Brady has some amazing ideas that I'm here to help make a reality. I have been so impressed with his vision." She looked at Brady. "And I am so grateful for the opportunity to be a part of it."

"I'm definitely the lucky one to have your help," he replied. His dimples appeared, making her whole day.

"What kind of *amazing ideas* are you trying to *make a reality* exactly?" Sabrina mocked. She seemed flustered.

"Well, I'm not sure who you are," Alexa said. "But I don't think we can tell you that." This woman wasn't going to act like she had a right to know anything about what Brady was up to. She had a fiancé she needed to focus on.

"We cannot," Brady affirmed. He picked up his glass and finished off his drink.

"I do promise that all of Apple Hollow will want to be a part of it when Brady gets things up and running. You're from around here, right?" She looked at the bearded guy, who nodded. "So I'm sure you'll hear about it when the time comes."

The server appeared with their food. Alexa's mouth watered at the sight of the burger that was put in front of her.

"It was good to see you two, but it looks like our lunch is served," Brady said.

Sabrina hesitated. She touched his shoulder. "I just wanted you to know that Dylan and I did not get back together until you and I were broken up. I know it seems like things are moving fast."

"I believe you," he replied, touching her hand. "I'm happy that you're happy. You know that's all I ever wanted."

The way his words physically impacted Alexa surprised her. She wished she had that kind of forgiveness in her heart for Brett. That she could sit there in front of him and his new person someday and tell him his happiness was all that mattered. She wasn't sure she'd ever be able to do that. Brady was a much better person than she was.

"It was nice to meet you," Alexa called after them as they walked away. Once they were out of earshot, she reached across the table and put her hand over his. "Are you okay?"

"That was awkward. Sorry."

"Don't you apologize to me. You are literally the most gracious person I have ever met. Remember when I was rambling about all those things that make you amazing? I'm adding extremely gracious to it."

"Stop. It's taken every ounce of self-control to not climb over this table to kiss you as it is, and we both know what your compliments do to me."

She had been the one to put an end to the kissing. Maybe that was stupid of her. Why was she denying them both the joy that came from giving in to the feelings they both clearly had? She did it because she knew it was going to be hard enough to say goodbye without adding more layers to these emotions. She did it because the more times she kissed him, the more ingrained in her memory his kissing ability would be, and then no one would ever compare.

Alexa picked up her burger and took a bite, needing something to distract her own mouth from these thoughts and feelings. She groaned.

"This is so good," she said once she swallowed it down.

Brady just grinned as he took his own bite. They ate their lunch and limited their conversation to the food and how good it was. He was a man of his word and let her split the bill with him. She could tell that he didn't like it, but it made her feel better to know that she was drawing that line. They needed lines because everything else about them was so fuzzy.

"All right, you've been fed and hydrated. Are you ready to go to the top of Maple Peak?"

"I would feel more confident in my answer if I knew how I was getting there."

Brady still wouldn't give in. He slid on his sunglasses and they exited the brewery. "Guess we're both going to have to wait for our questions to be answered."

Maple Peak turned out to be a ski resort. As they drove in, Alexa could easily make out the ski runs that cut through the trees on the side of the mountain. It reminded her of the way the baseball fields in Central Park stood out in the middle of all those trees when she looked at it from above.

"Why is a ski resort open in the summer?" she asked, trying to figure out what they were going to do here without any snow.

"In the summer, they offer gondola rides to the

top and some other activities on the mountain. I think you can take a ski lift halfway up. That's where they have a zip line, some rock-climbing walls, and other activities for kids. There are also hiking trails. If we had more time, we could hike up and down, but since we don't, we're going to ride up and hike down a trail that will take us by Bobcat Falls."

"Sounds like fun, Mr. Activities Director. I wish I had one of you in New York to entertain me when I don't have the energy to think of something fun to do."

"Well, I wish I had one of you here to help me figure out how to fill out that spreadsheet correctly, so we're even."

In a perfect world, they could have it all. But it wasn't a perfect world. Far from it. Alexa took a deep breath and tried to focus on the sweet-smelling pine instead of the ache in her chest. He offered to put her purse in the backpack he brought for the hike down. He had thought of everything—water, sunscreen, snacks, and a hat if she needed one, along with a sweatshirt in case she got a chill at the summit.

"I've already ordered us gondola tickets online, so you're going to have to accept my kindness and ride with me."

She didn't refuse him. It was nice to have someone want to take care of her. It was something that had been sorely missing from her marriage. Brett hadn't cared about what made her happy or what he could have done for her to lighten her load. He had only been focused on reiterating all the things she wasn't doing to make him happy, or how unhappy he was that she wasn't focused on taking care of him.

Brady was a breath of fresh air. The way he approached life and other people was exactly what Alexa needed to know existed in this world. For that, she would always be grateful to him.

They got on the gondola and somehow the mountain was even more beautiful from this vantage point. "How gorgeous is this in the fall?"

"I'm tempted to tell you that you'll have to come back and see it for yourself, but it's almost as gorgeous as the view of the valley on the ATV trail. I would say the ATV trails are the place to be to take in all the fall colors."

Imagining it was enough to make her want to come back to see it for herself. In fact, there was a part of her that wanted to revisit and take in all four seasons in New Hampshire. Brady had made it clear they each offered their own unique experiences. Of course, the biggest draw to coming back was a Seasons who didn't have anything to do with the time of year.

She knew she couldn't make any promises, though. It would be wrong to let him think that she could reappear in his life only to get too caught up in her work to ever make it back.

The pressure in her ears began to build the higher they got. When they arrived at the top, he helped her off the gondola.

"This is Maple Peak's summit," Brady said, holding his arms open wide. "We are now over four thousand feet up in the air and you have three-hundred-and-sixty-degree views. Isn't it awesome?"

Alexa loved how he loved everything about the places he took her to visit. This man was so full of positivity. He still managed to maintain a sense of wonder even though she knew he had been to all of these places time and time again.

They weren't the only ones up there. There were two families with kids and one group of women walking around and taking pictures.

"What do you usually do at the summit?" she asked, assuming getting there and down was the adventure part.

"Come here." He extended a hand. She took his hand and he led her to a lookout point. Brady pointed out some of the landmarks she was familiar with from this vantage point. He showed her where Lake Champney was and how the inn was partially hidden from view by the trees surrounding it.

After giving her time to take some pictures

with her phone, Brady guided her to the trail that would take them down the mountain. Purple, yellow, and white wildflowers were scattered along the edges of the trail. About halfway down, they crossed a footbridge that took them over the river. As they followed the trail, the rumbling of water rushing over rocks became louder than the sound of birds chirping and chattering.

The Bobcat Falls were loud. Water spilled over the ledge, white and foamy as it cascaded off the rocky terrain. The misty spray that filled the air at the bottom felt good against Alexa's skin. She closed her eyes and let her other senses take over. The sound of the falls was, to a city girl, something she would only hear on a relaxation app on her phone.

Brady leaned in close. "I like to come up here because it's a good place to let go of everything and anything that's been bringing me down."

Alexa opened her eyes. "How do you do that exactly?" she yelled over the din.

"I'll show you," he said before balling his hands into fists and tilting his head to the sky. "I am not an idiot! I am going to do something amazing! And please let Dylan cut himself shaving when he finally shaves off that beard!"

Alexa laughed at that last one. "What was that? Scream therapy? That helps?"

He looked at her as if surprised she didn't believe it. "Yeah, it does. Call it whatever you want, but you've got to try it."

"I wouldn't even know what to yell." She glanced around to see who might be looking at them after his little outburst. There was no one around. Still, there was no way she was going to scream something in front of this waterfall.

"Yes, you do. Come on. Let's get closer. No one will hear you except for the waterfall gods." He guided her off the trail and removed his backpack, setting it on the ground. "I don't want our stuff to get wet if you fall in and I have to jump in to save you," he said with a wink.

She cocked an eyebrow. No way was she falling in the water here. He laughed and pulled her along. They carefully moved closer to the falls, leaping from rock to rock. Brady stopped and held out a hand to help her join him on the same boulder.

He practically had to yell so she could hear him over the waterfall. "Whatever you wish you could say but have been too polite to let out, now's your chance to release it into the wind! Shout it to the heavens! I promise no one will hear you."

She hated that she was so self-conscious. She snuck a peek over her shoulder again. No one else had come down the trail.

"I promise it will feel good to let it go," he said, giving her shoulder a squeeze.

Why she wanted to scream was obvious. *What* she wanted to say that would rid her of the negativity she'd been carrying around since the divorce was not. She thought about the last time she had talked to Brett. It had only been several days ago, when she ran into that tree. The anger that had bubbled up after getting off the phone with him resurfaced.

She let go of her inhibitions and screamed at the cascading water. "I am not going to let myself cry over some jerk who never loved me the way I deserved!" She sucked in a deep breath, needing air after shouting so loudly. "I am not the bad guy! I deserve to be happy!"

"There you go! Feel better?" Brady asked.

She faced him and shook her head as the tears began to fall. Brady frowned sympathetically and wrapped his arms around her, pulling her against him. Instead of helping her release those emotions, they overwhelmed her, rising to the surface, where they smacked her across the face.

"I'm sorry. I didn't want to make you cry," he said into her ear. Of course, Brady would apologize, even though it was Brett, not Brady, who had hurt her.

She pressed her cheek against his shoulder. "He left me but wanted me to feel like it was all my fault. He stabbed me in the heart and twisted the knife. It wasn't enough that he was leaving, he wanted to make sure I understood that not only did he not love me anymore, I was the only one to blame."

Brady tightened his hold. "That's wrong and cruel. I'm sorry he did that to you."

"What's worse is I owned it. I blamed myself and my work schedule. I believed that I was unworthy of his love. I drove up here because I thought I needed to be someone different. Someone who didn't work twenty-four seven. Someone interesting. Someone he could have loved, but you know what I've realized?" She pulled back enough to look Brady in the eye. "I've realized that maybe it was him. Maybe if he hadn't been trying to force me into a life I wasn't ready for, I wouldn't have stayed at work to avoid him. Maybe if he asked me what I wanted, we could have compromised. But he didn't care about me. He didn't want me to be interesting. He just wanted me to be who he thought I should be."

Brady cupped her cheek. "He really blew it. He gave up the most interesting woman around. We confirmed that already."

He made her laugh in spite of all the other emotions consuming her. "When the first moose ran me off the road, he was alerted that I crashed a car and the only thing he had to say about it was that it was pathetic that I was trying to get his attention. He didn't even ask me if I was okay."

Brady's jaw tightened. "I strongly dislike this guy."

"You know what you asked me the very first time we met when I was momentarily stunned by how good-looking you are? You asked me if I was okay. I was glitching because a cute guy was talking to me and you wanted to make sure I was okay. I think that's why I like you so much." Letting all that out felt like removing a weight that she had been carrying around on her shoulders for over a year.

"I like you, too." Brady held her face with both hands and tipped up her head. "I'm going to kiss you again even though I know we said we weren't going to do that anymore."

Before Alexa could protest, which she had no plans to do, he kissed her. He wanted to stitch up her broken heart, and she was going to let him. Brady made everything better. He couldn't be hers forever, but he could be hers for right now.

When he let her go, all the anger and hurt she had felt raging at the waterfall about Brett had dissipated. It was like all those feelings were the same as the water running down the mountainside. First, it crashed against the rock, angry and aggressive. Then it splashed into the pool down below, making a commotion. Until it turned into a mist that only lightly clung to her hair, her clothes, her skin.

"I do deserve to be happy," she said as she tried to catch her breath.

Brady laughed and kissed her again. "All I want is for you to be happy."

She knew he was telling the truth because she saw it in his eyes. She felt it in his touch. Movement behind him caught her attention. Standing over their backpack was one very large...

"Moose!" She pointed at it nuzzling the backpack, probably trying to get the food in there.

Brady turned and Alexa had to move as he spun around. Her shoes had good traction, just not on a slippery, wet rock. It only took a second for her to hit the water and go under.

Not again.

CHAPTER SIXTEEN

"THE MOOSE AROUND here are out to get me. It's the only thing that makes sense."

Alexa was sure that there was no other reasonable explanation for these encounters. Brady saw it as another amazing addition to her moose stories. He had never known anyone to come that close to three different moose in one week. She should be asking him to stop at the gas station so she could buy some lottery tickets.

"I think it means you're the chosen one. They're drawn to you... It doesn't have to be a bad thing. I don't think you appreciate how unusual it is to see that many moose in the middle of the day in one week. They usually don't come out of the woods until after dusk. I think it's lucky."

"Says the guy who isn't sitting in wet underwear right now," she grumbled.

They turned into the Seasons Inn parking lot. Brady pulled up to the front door. "I'll drop you off here so you can get to your room as quickly as possible. We need you in some dry underpants as soon as possible."

Alexa snorted when she laughed. "Oh, my gosh, do not talk about my underwear and definitely do not call it *underpants*."

"You brought it up," he replied in his defense. He put the car in Park so she could jump out.

She opened the door and started to get out. "Thank you for taking me to lunch and showing me Maple Peak," she said when she was halfway in, halfway out. "Sorry about getting your car seat a little wet."

"Don't worry about it."

She climbed all the way out of the car and raced inside. She wasn't even that wet anymore. Between hiking the rest of the way down and changing into the spare shirt he'd brought, she was practically dry. The last thing he was worried about was his car. He was too focused on the fact that she was wearing his shirt. It made him happier than it should have. He also hoped she forgot to give it back and a little piece of him would go back to New York City with her.

Brady knew he shouldn't let himself fall for this woman, but it was too late. She had captured a very big piece of his heart in the short time that she'd been here. Hearing her process what happened at the end of her marriage solidified it. She deserved so much more love and appreciation than her ex had given her. Brady wished he could be the one to give it to her.

His phone chimed with a text as he made his way into the inn. Alexa had sent him a message.

I'm going to put my new ideas into your spreadsheet. Maybe we can finalize your presentation tonight?

She wanted to see him again today. A moose may have stomped on his backpack while trying to steal his trail mix, but he was the luckiest guy around. This smart, beautiful woman was helping him out and wanted more of his time and attention.

Quinn was standing in the middle of the lobby when Brady walked in. "Why do you look like that?"

"Like what?"

"So...*happy*. Do you have any idea what is going on around here?"

It took everything he had not to roll his eyes. Brady knew that there were issues going on, but it didn't mean that the inn's problems needed to become his problems. He was allowed to appreciate the joy in his own life.

"Is there something I can do to help? Are we going to put up the event tent?"

Quinn seemed taken aback by his willingness to pitch in. He must have been expecting a snarky reply. He had to shift gears. "We are putting it up tomorrow morning. It would be great if you could help. You've been MIA for a couple of hours. I wasn't able to ask you earlier," he said, unable to hold back the dig.

"Well, good thing you don't need me until tomorrow morning. I'll be there. Do you know where Dad is?"

"I think he went to talk to Mom in the kitchen. Why?"

"You're just full of questions for me today, brother." Brady patted his brother's upper arm. "Don't you have some guests to check in? Maybe a new reservation to take? I think the phone is ringing."

Quinn turned to see if anyone was standing by the front desk, and Brady took that distraction as his opportunity to escape and find his parents. They were right where Quinn thought they'd be. His mom was pulling some cupcakes out of one of the ovens and his dad was supervising while sitting at the prep table, drinking some iced tea.

"Just the people I was looking for," Brady said, garnering their attention.

His mom set the cupcakes on top of the cooling racks she had set up on the prep table. "You can't have any of these cupcakes, Brady."

"I wasn't going to take one of your cupcakes. At least not until they're frosted," he said with a waggle of his eyebrows.

She playfully scowled at him and wiped her hands on her apron. "What are you doing here then?"

"I was looking for Dad."

"I don't have any frosted cupcakes for you either, son," his dad joked. It was good to see he had his sense of humor. His dad's hair seemed to have a bit more gray in it today. All the stress lately was aging the poor guy.

"I was actually going to ask for some of your time, not your sweets."

"You can have all the time you need. You know that."

"I have a proposal. A real business proposal that I want to present to you. Could we do something tomorrow after we raise the event tent?"

"You have a proposal to present to me?"

"Can I hear this proposal?" his mom asked, leaning one hip against the table.

"I would love it if both of you listened to it."

His dad glanced over at his mom and they engaged in some kind of silent conversation. Mom nodded and his dad said, "I think it might be a good idea if we had the whole family there. Quinn and Nora as well."

Brady wasn't expecting such a large audience for his first-ever presentation. "Why do they need to be there?"

"We need to have a family meeting," his dad explained. "Your business proposal can be added to the agenda."

"I really wanted to run it by you before you ran it by Quinn. You know how he is—he tends to focus on the negatives. I need someone who is willing to listen with a positive spirit."

"I think it's important that everyone be involved," his dad said. "It will make more sense at the meeting."

Brady didn't like the sound of that. It wasn't often that they had family meetings about the inn. The few times they had all been summoned to talk about business, there had either been something really good or extremely bad going on. Given the state of things lately, this meeting was giving off some bad vibes. Brady didn't want bad vibes to ruin his presentation.

"Maybe we can go over it alone after the meeting."

His dad put a hand on Brady's shoulder. "It's going to be fine. You and your brother and your sister are going to need to figure out how to work together as a team. It's important."

It was clear that there was no way his dad was going to let this happen any other way. Quinn and Nora were going to have to hear his proposal. He needed Alexa to do her magic and make this presentation flawless.

"Fine, Seasons family meeting tomorrow morning after we get the tent up."

"Can you let your siblings know?"

Brady pulled out his phone and texted in the family group chat.

Family meeting at Dad's request tomorrow morning after the tent is up. Find coverage for the front desk.

His mom's phone chimed in her pocket, but the silence on his dad's side of the table obviously meant he wasn't carrying his around. It was a bad habit of his. He forgot that sometimes his phone was the easiest way for all of them to get a hold of him.

"You kids and your phones. Doesn't anyone talk face-to-face anymore?" his dad complained.

Brady shook his head. "Sometimes you act like you're ninety instead of sixty-five."

"Sometimes I feel like I'm ninety instead of sixty-five."

Brady's mom frowned at that comment. "You need to make sure you get a good night's sleep tonight. You've been burning the candle at both ends lately and it's taking a toll. You look a little flush."

She moved around the table to stand beside Gavin. Pressing the back of her hand to his forehead, she asked, "Did you eat some lunch today?"

"Quinn and I had a working lunch. I think we ate something while we were talking things over."

"That's not a very convincing yes, dear."

"My stomach's been acting up. I had some bad heartburn this morning after breakfast. Stop worrying about me. I'm worrying enough about everything else." He reached for her hand and gave it a squeeze. "That's enough worrying for one couple."

"I worry about you because I love you." She gave him a kiss on his forehead. "Deal with it."

Brady loved how his parents loved one another. They set the bar high for what to expect from the person he wanted to commit to spending the rest of his life with. Gavin and Laura Seasons always had each other's backs. They made all major decisions together and they trusted each other implicitly. No one was prouder of his dad than his mom, and no one raved about his mom more than his dad.

"I've got to take some guests zip-lining." Brady tried to take an unfrosted cupcake out of the pan, but his mom smacked his hand. "Jeez, I'll see you guys later."

BRADY AND ALEXA worked on the proposal all night. She had added all the new ideas they had brainstormed earlier in the day. Everything was put into a written report that he would hand out to each member of his family to read over. Alexa also wrote Brady notes to use with the slideshow presentation she made for him to accompany the written proposal. It was full of interesting visuals and graphics. Nora was going to love it. Quinn would find something wrong with it, but Brady was really proud of what they had accomplished.

They met up in her suite the next morning after Brady helped put up the event tent. His family was gathering in the conference room in fifteen minutes.

Brady clicked through the presentation one more time on his laptop. "This is perfect. It's like you took all the chaos in my head and organized it to come up with this slideshow."

"Your family is going to throw their full support behind this idea. You are going to do great."

Alexa's confidence helped more than she could imagine. He hadn't expected to feel so nervous. "Where do you think you're going to be when I'm finished? I'm going to want to tell you how it went when it's over."

"I was going to wait for you in the lobby on

one of those couches by the fireplace. Maybe I'll read a book. I need something to distract me."

Brady's anxiety made him antsy. He had to keep reminding himself this was his family—it wasn't a firing squad. They were going to be open to his ideas. They were going to see the hard work that he and Alexa had put into this and everything was going to go just the way he wanted it to.

He checked his watch. It was time to get downstairs. He couldn't be late when this was his show. "I gotta go."

She gathered up all the copies of the proposal they had printed out in the business office last night and handed them to him after he packed up his computer. "You've got this."

"Thank you so much for your help. I could not have done this without you."

She rested her palm against his chest. She could probably feel how fast his heart was beating. "You can thank me after you wow them and Quinn tells you it's the best idea he's ever heard."

"Let's not get too carried away."

"Your dad is going to love it." She gave him a chaste kiss on the cheek. "Go, so you're not late."

Alexa made him feel like he could do anything, and he was going to get his family to agree to host a Seasons at the Lake four times a year. He left the suite and took the elevator down to the main floor.

Everyone was already seated around the table when Brady came in. They had the conference-room phone set in the center of the table. Brady set down his stuff.

"Why do you have stacks of paper?" Quinn asked with a scrunched brow.

"I'm presenting to the family today." Brady began passing out the written reports.

"Hold on, Brady. Mom and I need to go over something first. We need to get Theo on the phone."

Theo was joining them? Theo never joined their family meetings about the inn. He didn't work there.

"Your mom texted him earlier that we'd be calling." Brady's dad tried to dial out on the conference-room phone but something wasn't working. His mom tried to help, then Nora jumped in.

"Why don't we just use my cell phone?" Quinn suggested, pulling out his phone and setting it on the table. "Clearly, we have a phone issue to worry about as well. This is great."

He called Theo, who answered on the third ring. "What's up, Quinn?"

"Family meeting time."

"What's with the emergency family meeting?"

Theo asked. He wasn't the only one wondering. "Is someone dying or something?"

"That's not funny," their mom said. "Never joke about that."

"Sorry, Mom. What's going on?"

"Your mom and I wanted to talk to the four of you because we have something important to share that impacts all of you."

Brady started to worry that maybe someone *was* dying. "Are both of you okay?"

"We're fine, sweetheart," his mom assured him. "But your father and I have been talking about the fact that we're getting older." She glanced over at their dad.

He reached for her hand. "We've decided that we're going to retire from running the inn."

The room went silent. Brady and Nora exchanged a look. They knew this was coming eventually, but they hadn't been expecting it so soon.

"Effective when?" Quinn asked.

"At the end of the year," their dad replied. Nora gasped. "But we have some issues to discuss."

"Some? There are a million issues to discuss," Quinn snapped. "You're going to retire when we're in the middle of a million disasters?"

"Hold up," Theo interjected. "Are you still

planning to be owners of the inn or is that why we're having a family meeting?"

"Obviously, the plan has always been to turn over equal ownership to the four of you. I know Quinn is feeling frustrated right now because the inn isn't in the best shape and there are a lot of bills that need to be paid, bills I don't want to burden you four with."

"How much money are we talking about?" Theo asked with a sigh that said he was going to write a check just because he could.

"This isn't about asking you for money, son."

"Well, if everyone is okay with me owning a bigger part of the inn but literally doing nothing to keep it up and running, I'll help you guys."

Brady was too overwhelmed to engage in this conversation. His dad and mom were going to retire. There was no way anyone was going to listen to his presentation after this conversation ended. Quinn looked like he was about to have a panic attack.

"It's not okay with me," Quinn argued. "I don't even think it's fair for him to get equal say in something that he has nothing to do with."

"Maybe he can be a silent partner," Nora suggested.

"There's always the option that all of you could decide to sell the inn," their dad said. "We know that it's a huge responsibility, not only operationally but financially."

Nora's face blanched. "We can't sell the inn."

"I'm not selling the inn," Quinn asserted.

"Let's sell," Theo said at the same time.

Brady didn't know what to say. He wasn't sure he could even speak if he wanted to. He had walked into this room expecting to talk to his family about how they could improve community relations, and instead there was a very real conversation going on about whether or not they would even own the inn by the end of the year.

The three siblings who could find their voices were all arguing. Nora and Quinn were adamant about not selling. Theo was reiterating what Quinn said that he couldn't afford to buy him out, so if Quinn wanted to sell his quarter, he could sell it to anyone if he wanted.

"Hey!" their dad shouted to get their attention. "No one needs to decide anything right now. I need you all to think about it. We're going to have to have several conversations moving forward because you all deserve to understand what is going on so you can make the best decision for you." His eyes began to water. "Of course, you know what this place means to me. You know I would love for it to stay in the family. At the same time, I know that by stepping down, I give up my right to make that decision."

"We don't want you to feel obligated to do anything. We also don't want you to feel like we're abandoning you with a money-pit situation," their mom said as Dad pulled out his handkerchief and wiped his eyes and then his sweating forehead.

Brady realized as he watched his dad that he actually felt chilled. Why was his dad sweating so much?

"You can't turn this over to us without some kind of clause that Theo can't sell his portion without the rest of us approving," Quinn said.

Theo was heated. "You can't tell me if I can sell my portion or not, Quinn. I can do whatever I want."

"Boys," their mom said in a warning tone.

Brady noticed his dad's breathing had changed. He seemed to be struggling to catch his breath. "Dad," he said, standing up. "Dad, are you okay?"

Everyone in the room shifted their attention to their dad. Brady made his way around the table. Their dad's face was beet red and his eyes started to flutter. He couldn't seem to get enough air to speak. "Call 911," Brady said to Quinn. "Dad, we're going to get you some help."

"What's going on?" Theo asked, his tone suddenly full of fear instead of anger.

"I'll call you back," Quinn said before ending the call and dialing 911.

Brady got him out of his chair and helped to lay him down on the floor. He held his dad's hand. "Try to slow your breathing down. You're panicking—it's making it harder. Follow me." Brady took a deep breath in and let it out as slowly as he could.

His dad was having a heart attack and Brady was sure his life was spiraling out of control.

CHAPTER SEVENTEEN

ALEXA HAD NEVER been so anxious for someone to come and tell her how a meeting went, and she had waited for many people to come out of some pretty serious meetings before. She wanted this so badly for him, though.

Brady was going to hit this out of the park. They had practiced the presentation over and over. He was amazing when he wasn't overthinking it. Of course, under pressure, he might be overthinking it.

She shook her head. He was going to be fine. What she needed to focus on was making sure the inn was going to be fine. She had her computer open on her lap and had been doing her best to find a solution to the problem that she had created by telling Jordan about the Seasons Inn. There was no way she could let this place be put on the auction block. Brady had big plans and she wanted his plans to see the light of day.

Jordan had sent her at least a dozen emails. He had been doing the same digging she had done before she arrived in New Hampshire. He kept requesting information from her, and she kept letting him receive her out-of-office auto response. The bad news was that the inn was vulnerable. They needed money and they needed it quickly. Anyone could take advantage of that kind of situation, not just Gatton Investments.

Her first line of defense was to lure Jordan in another direction. There had to be a better objective out there. If that didn't work, she would have to go against her own personal ethics and lie. At the very least, she would have to downplay the inn's potential. She had been going through all her old files, trying to find something that they could go with instead. After she figured that out, she would have to put something together for the Seasonses so they could be safe from anyone coming to take over the property.

Suddenly, she heard sirens outside the inn. Glancing up from her computer, she saw other guests milling around, exchanging looks and whispers about what could be going on. Seconds later, two paramedics came racing in with a stretcher. The young man who was covering the front desk came out from behind the counter to greet them.

"We got a call that someone's possibly having a heart attack," one of the paramedics said. The front-desk guy didn't seem to know what he was talking about and had no idea where to direct them.

Alexa put her own hand over her heart. How terrible. She wondered who it could be. There was that sweet, little old couple who always ate breakfast near her in the mornings. She hoped it wasn't either one of them.

Nora sprinted out of the hallway that led to the conference room, looking panic-stricken. "Back here! Please, hurry!"

Alexa jumped to her feet, a sense of dread grabbing hold of her. Why wasn't Nora listening to Brady's presentation? She tried to rationalize it, calm her worried heart. Maybe someone had called her out of the meeting because of the guest in distress. The alternative was too horrible to consider.

She needed to see Brady. Just as she thought his name, he came from the same hallway, followed by his entire family, except for his dad. His mom was in tears and Quinn's grimace was worrisome. The paramedics followed and pushed the patient into the lobby. Mr. Seasons was lying on the stretcher wearing an oxygen mask. Alexa's stomach dropped.

Brady's eyes locked on hers and she saw the raw fear in them. She ran to him and he wrapped her up in his arms. "I think he had a heart attack," he barely choked out around the emotion lodged in his throat.

"Oh, Brady." She hugged him tighter. This was the way she'd expected to greet him when he came out of that room, but it was supposed to be in celebration, not whatever this was. He didn't speak, he simply clung to her. She wasn't going to let go until he did.

"Mom is going with the ambulance," Nora said, coming up beside them. "We're going to have to drive separately."

Brady released his hold on Alexa. His sister was too upset about her dad to ask questions about why Brady was hugging a guest.

"I'll drive." Quinn appeared with keys in his hand. He didn't even seem to notice Alexa standing there.

There was a moment when she thought she should step away and give the family their privacy to figure out what they needed to do, but Brady immediately reached for her.

"Will you come with me?" His usually smiling eyes were pleading and sad.

There was no hesitation. It didn't matter what his brother and sister would think. If Brady wanted her there, she was going to be there. She nodded and went to get her things from the couch.

Quinn and Nora exchanged a look but didn't

say anything as Brady and Alexa followed them to the car. In the back seat of Quinn's SUV, Brady's leg was bouncing out of control. She'd never seen him wound so tight. Quinn made eye contact with Alexa through the rearview mirror. There were no words exchanged, but it was clear that he had a million questions.

"He's going to be fine. He's going to be fine," Nora repeated over and over.

Brady held Alexa's hand in a death grip the whole way to the hospital. They followed behind the ambulance until they had to turn into the parking lot. The ambulance went straight to the entrance, where medical personnel met them to unload Mr. Seasons.

Alexa followed Brady in silent support. The tiny waiting room in the Apple Hollow Hospital was nothing like a busy ER in New York City. There were only two other people waiting to be seen. Three rows of brown plastic chairs filled the space. A stack of magazines sat on an end table in the corner. There was that familiar antiseptic smell, however.

Brady didn't sit. He motioned for Alexa to do so and then started pacing back and forth. Nora sat next to Alexa, and Quinn went to the nurse's desk to let them know they were there for their dad, who had just come in via ambulance. Their mom wasn't allowed to stay with her husband, so she joined them, sitting next to her daughter.

"Is there a reason why we brought a guest to the hospital with us?" Quinn finally asked when he crossed Brady's path and took a seat on the other side of his mom.

"Alexa is my friend," Brady replied. "I asked her to come because I don't know if you noticed, but I'm kind of freaking out."

"We're all freaking out, but don't you think this is a private matter?"

"I don't care what you have to say about it, Quinn. I want her here and she agreed to come. What does it matter to you?"

"Boys, I can't listen to you fight right now," their mom interrupted. She fidgeted with her hands, turning her wedding ring around and around. "Please, stop."

Quinn reached over and held her hand. "Sorry."

"If it wasn't for Brady, we might not have got him here in time. You did such a good job staying calm and taking action," his mom said to him.

"I didn't even realize what was happening," Nora said.

"I hadn't been paying attention to all the signs," their mom said. "He hasn't been sleeping well. He was sweating all the time. I should have noticed and made him go get checked out."

"Don't do that, Mom," Nora said, putting a comforting hand on her mom's back. "There was no way you could have known what was going to happen."

Brady linked his fingers behind his head. "I noticed the sweating, too. I should have said something."

"The same goes for you. There was no way you could have known. You're not a doctor," Nora said. "But he's with the doctors now, and he's going to be fine. Everyone needs to believe that."

"I should call Theo back," Quinn said, standing up and tapping on his phone. "He's texted me a million times."

While Quinn called their other brother, Alexa watched Brady. He was a bundle of nerves. She wasn't sure what she could do to distract him.

"You're leaving tomorrow, aren't you?" Nora asked Alexa.

"I am. I've had the best time. Your inn is so lovely and everyone is so accommodating. I can't say enough nice things about it."

Nora tried to smile. "We're happy to hear that. I didn't realize you and Brady had become so close. I guess it was all those activities I signed you up for."

"That definitely played a part. I also helped him write up the proposal he was presenting today. I was hoping to hear all about how much you loved his ideas before I had to go back to New York. Something tells me he didn't get through much of it before things went south."

"We didn't even get to Brady's proposal," Nora said. She glanced up at Brady. "Other family business took precedence."

"You worked on the proposal with Brady?" his mom asked, lifting her head.

"She does this kind of stuff for a living," Brady explained. "She offered to help me when I told her I was having a hard time convincing Dad to listen to my ideas."

"But Brady is one hundred percent the mastermind behind all of it. I was basically his sounding board and his scribe. Hopefully, Mr. Seasons will make a full recovery and get another chance to hear Brady out."

"Ha! It doesn't even matter what Dad thinks anymore," Brady said, throwing his hands up. "Now I guess I have to appeal to Quinn, who hates everything, and Theo, who wants nothing to do with anything. My presentation should be a smashing success."

"Don't say that," his mom pleaded. "Your dad is still going to be involved. I know we threw you guys for a loop, but you know how your dad feels about the inn."

Alexa was confused. She wasn't sure if Brady

was worried that his dad wasn't going to recover or if something else was going on.

Nora seemed to read her mind. "My parents announced some big news about their retirement right before all this happened with my dad."

Alexa's business-minded brain kicked into action. "Is the plan to turn the inn over to your children?" Alexa asked Mrs. Seasons.

"That's the plan. Of course, my children never want to make anything easy."

"The only one not making things easy is Theo, but what's new about that?" Quinn said as he returned. "He wants to talk to you, Mom." He handed her the phone.

That same sinking feeling from before came over Alexa. More drama with the inn. Alexa didn't think things could get worse, but they kept finding a way. Transferring ownership from two people to four. One sibling who didn't want anything to do with the inn. Jordan would be celebrating if he heard about it.

All a potential investor had to do was throw some money at Theo. They could offer to bail them out of trouble by assuming the loan and in return ask for controlling interest. Once that happened, it would all be over. Given the current financial predicament the inn was in, it would be so easy.

Brady had a hand in his hair, pulling his hair

and scratching his scalp. The usually positive and sunny guy she had gotten to know over the last week was a ball of anxiety.

Alexa stood. "What if we got drinks for everyone?" she asked, looking at Brady. "Will you come with me to get some water? Is everyone good with water?"

The other three Seasonses nodded and thanked her. It was Alexa's turn to take Brady by the hand and lead the way. They found a small alcove with vending machines. Brady leaned against the snack machine while Alexa got out some money to buy the waters.

"I thought he was going to stop breathing before the ambulance got there. I thought I was going to have to do CPR on my own dad."

Alexa stopped what she was doing and gave him another hug. "I'm so sorry that you had to even think about that. I can't imagine. It sounds like you did everything you could to get him here. He's in good hands, like your sister keeps saying."

He leaned into her. She was glad she could be there for him today like he had been there for her yesterday. She hoped that her presence would be enough.

"Sorry for being such a wreck," Brady said, straightening.

"You are not a wreck. You once told me to cut

myself some slack for being a normal human with feelings. You need to take your own advice. Let's get some water." Alexa went back to the vending machine.

"I guess I just feel like I went from being on top of the world to the bottom in one hour. When I left your suite, I thought I was finally going to prove to my family that I could contribute to the business in a different way."

"You're still going to get your chance, Brady."

"You don't understand. My dad and mom dropped that bomb on us and Quinn started having a meltdown. Nora and I were in shock. Theo wanted to know how quickly he can get rid of his twenty-five percent because he doesn't want any of the headaches that Quinn was melting down about. All I could think was, I'm never going to get a chance to share my proposal because who knows what's going to happen in the next six months? And then, *boom*! My dad has a heart attack."

"Your brother can't sell." She didn't mean to turn this into a business-planning conversation, but she needed him to understand how important that was if they were going to maintain ownership. "It's imperative that the four of you stay united on this."

"I can't think about that right now," he said,

taking one of the water bottles from her. "I just want to know that my dad is going to be okay."

She was going to let him worry about his dad while she worried about setting them up for success in the future. They went back to the family and passed out the drinks. Alexa sat back down and pulled a notebook from her bag. She started jotting down the things that were the most pressing for the business so she could share them with him later.

A nurse stepped out into the waiting room. "Seasons? Is there anyone here for Gavin Seasons?"

Mrs. Seasons raised her hand and got to her feet. "Here!"

The nurse explained that she could come back and sit with him. Due to his level of care, only one person was allowed back there right now. Once they had things under control, the other visitors were welcome to sit with him.

Brady was not a fan of having to stay in the waiting room. Alexa needed to find him a better distraction than pacing the linoleum.

"You know, I have my laptop. If you wanted, you could show Nora and Quinn your presentation. It's something to do while you wait."

He stopped moving for a second, considering her offer. "I don't know. No one is in the right mindset."

"It could be a nice distraction," Nora said. "Maybe that's what we need."

Brady looked to Quinn, who was scrolling on his phone. "What about you? Do you want to go over my proposal while we wait?"

Quinn shrugged. "I guess there's nothing else to do. I hope you're well prepared, though. If we're going to have a bigger stake in everything, I'm not willing to do anything that hasn't been well-thought-out."

"This is very well-thought-out. Your brother considered everything and he has specific plans for how to make it all come together," Alexa said in Brady's defense.

She opened the presentation and handed her laptop over to Brady. "You've got this."

Brady sat down in the spot their mother had vacated in between Quinn and Nora. He clicked around and started selling the four Seasons at the Lake to them. He didn't even have his presentation notes out but was going off his memory instead. Alexa smiled as he remembered it exactly like they had practiced.

Every so often Alexa would chime in to elaborate or to help answer a question one of the siblings would ask, but Brady was the star of the show. When he finished, Nora even clapped.

"That is awesome, Brady. I love everything about it," Nora said. "It fits our brand so perfectly. I can't believe we didn't think of it before."

Quinn had gone quiet. He reached over and clicked to go back a couple slides. "All of these numbers are legit? You checked with all these people?"

"Everything you see here we researched this week. I called everyone or went and talked to them face-to-face. I made every effort to make sure that you had all the data you needed to make an informed decision."

"I'm not going to lie..." Quinn began. There was a long pause. Alexa could see Brady losing faith. He had done all this work, and she could tell he was jumping to the conclusion that Quinn was preparing to tear it to shreds. His brother surprised him, though. "You two did a good job."

There was no way she was going to share the credit or let Quinn make Brady feel like this wasn't the product of his creativity and hard work. "This was mostly Brady. He deserves all the credit."

"There's no way Brady thought to check with the clerk's office about the permits."

Brady shot Alexa a look that said, *I told you.* He certainly knew his brother quite well. He called it and she smiled, acknowledging he was right.

"I asked the right person for help... What can I say? She knew exactly what potential costs we needed to look into that I hadn't considered. She spent a lot of hours going over things with me. I really couldn't have done it without her."

"It's a fun project. I was happy to help," she assured him. She hadn't realized until she worked on this with him that it was much more satisfying to generate a positive outcome for a company than to expose all the negatives.

"Come on, there has to be something in it for you," Quinn challenged. "What are we missing here? Do you work for someone who is going to make some money off this idea?"

Alexa shook her head. "No."

"Can't people do things to be nice? Does there always have to be some kind of payoff?" Brady snapped.

"There was a payoff. I got to help someone I care about," Alexa said. They had to realize that there was something going on between the two of them. She was literally sitting in the ER waiting room with them. She didn't see any other "friends" hanging around. "I consult with a lot of businesses. I can tell you that I believe this will be an awesome opportunity for the Seasons Inn. I think we've shown that there is some nice potential for it to generate short- and long-term revenue."

"Lord knows we need revenue," Quinn said, rubbing his forehead. "I think you should show this to Dad when he gets out of this place, Brady. I think he's going to love it."

Alexa wished she'd had her phone out to capture the expression on Brady's face when Quinn shared that compliment. It was a mixture of shock and pride. That was the look she had been hoping to see when she had been in the lobby, waiting for him to come out of the meeting.

"You would give your stamp of approval?" Brady asked, still obviously unsure he could trust his ears.

"It's a well-thought-out plan. It's not missing anything. You even included things I'm not sure I would have identified as probable costs and possible revenue opportunities. It's really good, Brady."

It took a minute, but Alexa could tell that Brady finally let that sink in. His shoulders relaxed and the crinkling by his eyes appeared as the smile returned to his face. This was the moment she had wanted for him.

Her phone rang, stealing her attention. She glanced at the screen. Neil, her assistant, was calling. He had not bothered her since the very first day of her vacation. She wanted to ignore it, but her curiosity got the best of her. She excused herself to take the call.

"Hey, Neil. What's going on?"

"It's not Neil. It's Jordan. You weren't answering my calls so I had to get creative."

Alexa saw red. How dare he put Neil in that position. "Jordan, this is my last full day of vacation. I'll be back in New York tomorrow. Can you not respect this one boundary?"

"What is all that New England air doing to you? Where's the Alexa I know who would be working day and night to get this new proposal done? The Alexa I know would have cut her vacation short the second she found out that we lost Steel Masters. I thought you didn't because you were getting good intel, but you haven't responded to any of my questions, you haven't shared anything you've learned."

"We're going to have to shift gears, Jordan. I know what it looks like on paper, but they have no interest in selling. They don't need any outside investors. They want to keep it in the family and they have family with enough funds to make that happen."

She could hear Jordan put down the phone and curse up a storm. She was lying, but what else could she do? The only way to get Jordan to stop digging was to make him believe there was no gold. If she had to exaggerate Theo's willingness to help the family business, that was what she had to do.

"You didn't think about communicating that to me as soon as possible?"

"I just found out," she lied again. "I have another idea. When I get back to New York, we'll go over it."

"This is a nightmare, Alexa."

"Don't be so dramatic. Enjoy your weekend. I'll see you on Monday." She hung up and made her way back to the waiting room. The look on Brady's face made her blood turn to ice. When his gaze lifted and met hers, she knew something very bad had happened.

CHAPTER EIGHTEEN

THE FEELING OF earning Quinn's approval was even better than Brady had dreamed. If he could impress his older brother, he could do anything. "When we get back to the inn, we can look at the written proposal together," he said. "I think if we can get Dad on board, the ice rink will want to sponsor one of the winter activities. They like to boast that Theo started skating there. Maybe they can throw some support our way."

He clicked out of the presentation, looking for the file with the written proposal. On Alexa's desktop was a file named Seasons Inn. He figured that had to be the file that contained all of the work she and Brady had worked on over the last couple of days.

Only that wasn't what he found.

There were copies of public records regarding the land his dad owned, various financial records. Not only was Alexa looking into the inn, but she had also gotten a hold of his dad's personal information. There was a spreadsheet documenting what she knew, what she needed to know, and a list of the issues they were facing, like the renovation needs.

"What the heck is all that stuff?" Quinn asked, taking notice when Brady clicked on a document stating they missed a payment for their property taxes.

Brady's heart started pounding. All the positive vibes he'd felt a few minutes ago were gone and replaced by total dread. "I don't know. Why would she have all this stuff about the inn on here?"

"Who is this woman, Brady? Who does she work for and how did she get all this information?" Quinn's anxiety wasn't helping to ease Brady's.

Nora had her phone out and started googling Alexa. "'Alexa Fox, analyst for Gatton Investments,'" she said, reading off her professional page.

"Gatton Investments? As in Roger Gatton? Oh, my gosh, Brady. I hope you didn't tell her anything that was going on. Of course, we just told her Dad and Mom are retiring and that Theo wants nothing to do with the inn. This is fantastic!" Quinn exclaimed, as if it was anything but fantastic.

"Who's Roger Gatton?" Brady asked. "Is it bad that she works for him?"

"Roger Gatton, investor and developer," Nora explained from her phone.

"Come on, you two." Quinn always got flustered when his brother and sister showed that they weren't as knowledgeable about the business world as he was. "He's a huge corporate raider in New York. He buys companies and dismantles them for his own profit. If she works for Gatton, she was here to see if we're in need of an investor."

"We kind of are." Brady had heard enough of their conversations to know there wasn't enough money to pay for the bills and the renovations that needed to be done. She could be trying to help.

"He doesn't invest and let you keep the company, Brady. He invests, takes over, and, in our case, would probably tear down the inn and sell the property to the highest bidder."

Brady shook his head. That was not the way she talked about the inn when they spent hours brainstorming ways to bring in revenue. "Alexa wouldn't do that. She would not want anyone to tear the inn down."

"You've known this woman all of one week. How would you know what her real intentions are?"

Brady wanted to defend Alexa and their relationship. It had only been a week, but they had connected like he had never connected with anyone before. But there was that niggling of doubt. What if she was just doing her job? Why would she have all this information if she didn't plan to use it?

He looked up and there she was. She had taken a call. Maybe it was Jordan from work. Maybe this was why Jordan kept calling her all week. Maybe she and Jordan were working together to buy the inn out from under him. He pictured the two of them laughing at how stupid he was for not realizing that she was using him.

"Is your dad okay?" she asked, misreading the horrified expressions they were all wearing.

Brady closed the laptop and asked her to come with him. He couldn't have this conversation in front of Nora and Quinn. He went outside and she followed, confusion creasing her forehead.

He wasn't even sure where to start. Part of him didn't want to ask any questions, because as soon as he did, he would get answers and everything was going to change.

He loved her green eyes. Rings of blue, the color of the sky, mixed with the green like a watercolor painting. He didn't want to hate those eyes. He had stupidly given himself permission to fantasize about a future where he got to look into them for the rest of his life. Circumstances were already taking her away, but it was something else to not *want* to ever see her again. He didn't want to feel that way. He wanted to miss her, not hate her.

"What's the matter? You were so happy a few minutes ago."

He took a deep breath and forced the question out of his mouth. "Did you come to Apple Hollow to get information on the inn to give to your boss so he could invest in the inn and take it over?"

A tiny bit of him hoped she would start laughing, tell him that was the wildest thing she had ever heard, but her silence and the way her face fell told him all he needed to know.

"Brady—" she began but he held up a hand to stop her.

He handed her the laptop. "I need you to go get your bag while I call for someone to pick you up. I can't have you here with my family. Not when we are scared to death that our dad isn't going to make it. We can't sit with you, knowing you want to take our inn away from us."

She shook her head, vehemently denying what he knew to be true. "I don't want to take your inn. I am doing everything I can so *no one* can take the inn from you."

"I don't believe you, Alexa. There's a file on your computer with some very detailed documents that tells me different. The fact that you work for a company that invests in other companies to sell them off tells me different."

"I know that looks bad. I know what you saw. I was considering the inn for a potential takeover, but that was before I met you, before we became—"

"Do not say *friends*. I don't believe you." He tried to stop his voice from shaking. "You wrote down things I told you when I thought we were friends. You put that information into that file. I can't believe you would do that, but I also can't believe you when you say it's not true. Please go get your bag. I will have someone pick you up."

He did his best not to watch her wipe the tear that rolled down her cheek. He texted Kayden to come pick her up as his heart thundered in his chest. He couldn't afford to feel bad for her. His feelings were already too mixed up. His natural instinct was to soothe, to reassure.

Please go inside. Please go inside.

Finally, he heard the *swoosh* of the automatic doors opening as she went to get her things. It was a relief and a disappointment at the same time. If it wasn't true, she would have tried harder to convince him.

How was he going to protect his family from this? How was he going to protect the inn from the vultures who had been clearly circling all this time? Why did she help him write that business proposal if she was planning to ruin everything? That just didn't fit with the person he thought he knew.

Alexa returned with her bag hanging off her shoulder. He walked around her, making sure to keep his distance. "Kayden should be here in a couple minutes to take you back to the inn."

"I promise you that I will not let anyone take the inn away from your family. I do not want that to happen. You changed my life, Brady."

He walked back into the ER without a reply. He couldn't listen to her baloney. There was a huge mess to clean up and he had no idea where to begin. *Changed her life*. Her saying that made his blood boil. He thought she had changed his life for the better only to find that she was plotting to take away everything he loved.

Quinn and Nora were sitting where he had left them. He couldn't sit. It felt like he had enough adrenaline running through his body for ten men. "I didn't know. I know that's not a good excuse and it doesn't help us, but it's the truth."

"This is why we don't make friends with the guests." Quinn had to make it seem like all this could have been avoided if he had simply followed company policy. No company policy was going to convince his heart to not be drawn to her. There was no way to stop the chemistry that he thought existed.

"Don't do that to him," Nora said. "This isn't your fault, Brady. She spent time talking to all of us. I told her things, Quinn told her things, I'd bet Dad told her things, thinking her questions were innocent. She seemed so nice. I can see why you fell for her."

That last part snagged on his heart. "What do you mean I fell for her? Fell for her tricks?"

Nora cocked her head. "Come on, Brady. I was determined to make a match for her and I did it. I just didn't realize it was with my brother."

Brady shook his head. "I didn't fall for her. We were working on the Seasons at the Lake proposal. That's it."

"You two never kissed?" Nora challenged.

There was no way she knew that. No one had ever seen them kiss. It caused him physical pain to remember those times they had. Those would be the first memories he would wash away if he could.

"Great," Quinn said, pinching the bridge of his nose. "You were running around all week making out with a guest. Did you watch *any* of the professional-standards videos we require employees to watch every year?"

Nora burst out laughing. If Brady hadn't felt like his heart had been ripped out of his chest, he might have laughed as well.

All three of their phones chimed with a text.

It was their mom letting them know they could come back and see their dad.

"Don't tell Mom and Dad," Brady said, feeling like he was ten years old again, trying to stay out of trouble. This was no baseball through the window, though.

"I'm not doing that to Dad right now," Quinn said. "We need to act like everything is fine until we know he's going to be okay. Once that happens, you're the lucky one who gets to tell Dad everything."

Acting like things were fine sounded like a solid plan. A little impossible, given that Brady wasn't sure he'd be fine at all. This felt like a betrayal that would haunt him forever.

A nurse directed them where to go, and to their surprise, their dad was sitting up in bed, munching on some graham crackers. Their mom was fussing with the blanket they had draped over him. He was hooked up to a machine that monitored his vital signs. Nothing was beeping or alerting them that there was any concern.

Nora was the first one to speak. "How are you feeling?"

"Turns out it wasn't a heart attack. It was an anxiety attack," Dad replied.

"And if he doesn't reduce his anxiety, he's going to give himself a heart attack, so we're going to be making some changes at home and work," their mom said sternly. She threw away his cracker wrapper.

"The nurse is finishing up with my discharge papers. Are we all going to fit into the car?"

Brady should have been relieved, but he still didn't feel comfortable with this plan. "They're sending you home? Are they sure it wasn't a heart attack? It looked like an attack to me."

"They ran all the tests. None of them showed I was having a heart attack. There's no reason to keep me, and we don't need to be racking up hospital bills."

"We're glad you're okay, Dad," Quinn said. "You gave us all a scare."

Their dad waved a dismissive hand. "There's nothing to worry about. I need to make more time for relaxing, that's it."

"We only have one car. I think the three of us should head back to the inn and make sure all hell hasn't broken loose." Quinn looked to his mom. "We can send someone to pick you up when he's discharged."

"That's a good idea. We have a wedding today. We all need to show our faces and make sure everything goes smoothly after asking them to change their plans once already."

So much for relaxing. Here he was planning his workday already. Brady would never understand how the other men in the family could switch in and out of work mode so effortlessly. The last thing he was thinking about was what was happening back at the inn. Maybe that was why Alexa had targeted him. He was the weak link.

Nora gave their dad a hug. "Never do that to us again," she said.

Their mom sat down and furrowed her brow. "Where's Alexa?"

The three siblings all exchanged a look. It was Brady's fault she was there; it would be his responsibility to explain. "She had to go back to the inn."

"I was telling your dad that she helped you put together your business proposal."

"And that you two seem to be a bit cozy. What's that all about?" Dad asked. "I thought we had a chat about keeping things professional."

"He talked to you about her and you still crossed the line?" Quinn huffed.

Nora pushed open the curtains. "Maybe Quinn and I will head back and Brady can stay and explain what he's been up to the last week. Come on, Quinn."

Brady couldn't decide what would be worse, leaving with his brother and sister and listening to Quinn complain about what happened, or staying with their parents and explaining how he had let the fox inside the henhouse.

There was only one choice. He had to face his dad and mom and tell them what happened. "I made a mistake and I allowed my feelings to put us in a potentially bad spot."

His dad's bushy eyebrows pinched together. "What kind of bad spot?"

"Turns out Alexa works for a company that invests in struggling businesses so it can take them over and make a profit. She came here to gather information about the inn and what weaknesses they could exploit. Not knowing that was what she was doing, I allowed her to hear things and know things we don't usually share with guests."

"Oh, Brady," his mom said with a sigh.

"What kind of things?" his dad asked.

"All the electrical issues, the roof, the AC, the fact that you're retiring, and that maybe Theo doesn't want any part of all this trouble." He bit down on his bottom lip. That wasn't an exhaustive list, but it was damaging enough.

Brady glanced at the machine that was monitoring his dad's vitals to make sure he hadn't just caused him to have another attack.

His dad sat, processing. He scratched the back of his head. "Well, it sounds to me that now that we know someone's coming for us, we can plan accordingly."

"I promise to do whatever it takes to make sure no one takes over the inn."

"I'm not worried about that. I'm worried about you. That had to be a blow. You've been taking a lot of those lately."

His parents must have heard about Sabrina and Dylan and their upcoming wedding and baby. Nora hadn't been shy about sharing. What happened with Alexa wasn't the same as Sabrina. Things with Alexa were always temporary. It also wasn't like they had been together for years. He barely knew her. It was better that he found out that what he did know wasn't real right away.

"I'll be fine," Brady said, ignoring the way his whole chest felt tight.

He avoided his mom's stare. He knew she was looking at him with that motherly intuition that he was lying to himself. If he was, he wasn't going to acknowledge it. Alexa had been planning to betray him. There was no reason to mourn the loss of someone like that. Gatton Investments had no idea who they were messing with. The Seasonses wouldn't go down without a fight.

CHAPTER NINETEEN

THE DAY THAT Brett had announced he was leaving used to be the worst day of Alexa's life. Somehow, hearing a man she had only known for one week tell her he didn't believe her and wanted her to leave managed to be worse.

Honesty was something Alexa prided herself on. She believed in being ethical in her business practices. It was the accountant in her. Yet, she had bent the truth over and over again this past week. She had lied by omission and that was no better than telling a lie outright.

After being dropped off at the inn, she ran up to her suite and immediately got to work. There was a possibility that no one would care what she had to say, but she had to try. She would not let anyone take advantage of the Seasonses. The best way to do that was to arm them with the information they needed and some simple changes they could make to protect their assets. She was going to point out what their weaknesses were so they could shore things up and keep people like Jordan from swooping in and talking them into something that would not benefit them in the end.

She couldn't bring herself to leave the suite, calling for room service instead of taking the chance that she might bump into Brady. As much as she wanted to convince him that she wasn't trying to ruin his life, she also didn't want to cause him any more distress. He had been so worried about his dad, and instead of being his lifeline, she had pushed him over the edge.

Alexa rubbed her forehead as she reread what she had written so far. If she could just get one of the Seasonses to believe her intentions were good, maybe they would be safe from financial predators. The only other thing she could do was find a new lead for Jordan, but after everything that had happened, she could see a real person behind each and every company on her list. The tech company that was created by a twenty-two-year-old computer whiz was an excellent candidate, but all she could think about was how hard the young man had worked to make his business a reality. Her thoughts kept drifting to how she could help him maintain control of it so he could benefit from the expansion, not someone else.

It was as if she couldn't do her job anymore. Thinking about the people behind the business was messing with her head. She thought about how good it felt to work with Brady on his proposal and the joy she felt when he won his family over. It was better than any big takeover she had been a part of.

That was just one of the ways Brady had changed her life. She slumped over and let her head fall into her hands. Everything had gone from good to terrible in the blink of an eye. Her chest ached, knowing there wasn't enough time to repair the damage.

The next morning, Alexa rolled her suitcases to the door of her suite. She had contacted the car-rental company and the car she had damaged was fixed and ready to be driven back to New York. All she needed was a ride into town to pick it up. She glanced around to make sure she hadn't left anything behind. Her gaze lingered on the couch where she had sat with Brady, laughing, brainstorming, creating, kissing. She let the sting of knowing that would never happen again sink in.

A knock on the door startled her. She hadn't called down for help with her things, afraid that Quinn would answer the phone. Maybe they sent someone up to get her out of there. Suddenly, the fear set in that it could be Brady.

She decided it was best to rip off the bandage and open the door regardless of who was on the other side. To her surprise, Gavin Seasons stood there in his blue polo and khaki pants, looking much better than the last time she had seen him.

"Oh, I am so glad to see you're well! You are well?"

"I'm good, thank you. I'm sorry I caused such a commotion yesterday." Gavin was an older version of his son with his warm brown eyes and easy smile.

"Your family was so worried. I am so relieved that you're okay."

"Well, I appreciate that. I know you're checking out this morning, but I hoped that I could have a minute of your time."

The relief was quickly replaced by dread. Alexa stepped back and motioned for him to come on in. There was no way the owner of the inn was simply there to make sure she had a nice visit.

"Oh, the Garden Suite is one of my favorite rooms. Did you enjoy your stay?" he asked.

Her heart was thumping as he came in and walked over to the sitting area. "It was lovely. I have had the most wonderful time here."

"I'm glad to hear that, but I would actually like to talk to you about something else."

So much for the small talk. Alexa supposed she should be glad he didn't drag it out. "Of course. I think I know why you're here."

Gavin took a seat on one of the chairs opposite the couch. "I wanted you to know that I appreciate what you did for Brady. I read through his proposal last night when I got back from the hospital. It's a clear plan with some impressive details. If things work out and we can put his ideas into practice, it could be a great thing for the inn and the whole community."

"That's what I love about it." Alexa rubbed her palm over her heart. She sat down on the couch. "It really encapsulates all that Apple Hollow has to offer. I think it has amazing potential to be good for so many people and businesses in the area."

"See, that's what makes me so confused." He crossed his leg, resting his ankle on his knee. "I believe you when you say that. I see it on your face. So it makes me wonder why would you go through all that if you're planning to help someone do a hostile takeover?"

Alexa knew that was coming. She hoped that Gavin would understand. "I do not want to help anyone take this place from any of you. Before I got here, I was doing a profile on the inn. It's what I do. I work all the time. It's a terrible habit, and it's probably the reason I'm unhappy. But after I arrived and I let myself enjoy my vacation, I couldn't imagine this place being owned by anyone but your family. It should always be owned by your family."

"That didn't have anything to do with my son?" Gavin lifted an eyebrow.

The question sent her heart racing once again. She swallowed down the lump in her throat. "Brady is a very special person. I have never met anyone like him. He is the kindest and funniest guy I know. I love being around him because he loves life so much."

"He's the kind of guy who makes everything fun," Gavin said. "Why do you think I gave him the activities-director job? He's perfect for it."

"He really is," Alexa agreed. "He made this vacation what it was for me."

Gavin nodded. "I just needed to hear for myself what was going on. I don't think you've got some sinister plan to take over my inn, Ms. Fox."

He stood up and Alexa jumped up as well. "I swear that I don't, but I do want to warn you that you are in a very vulnerable position. I may be able to steer Gatton Investments away, but I can't guarantee that someone else looking for some land might not see this place as a gold mine."

"I get it. I have put this place at risk. I don't want to leave a mess for my kids to clean up."

"There are some simple things you can do to protect yourself and the inn from future investors who come snooping around. I started putting together some things to consider. I haven't figured out how to share them with you because

I didn't think Brady would listen to me. I know you have no reason to trust me, but I feel confident that if you follow the steps I've laid out, you'll be able to keep the inn in the family as long as you want it to be in the family."

"I'd be happy to look over whatever you want to share." Reaching into his pocket, he pulled out his wallet. He slid out a business card and handed it to her. "You can email me."

She pressed the card to her chest, overwhelmed that he was willing to listen to her. "I will. Thank you so much."

He gave her a quizzical look. "You're welcome?"

"For giving me a chance to redeem myself. At least in Brady's eyes."

"Sometimes we think we know what we're doing and then life throws us a curveball that makes us reconsider. I believe you reconsidered."

She had. Brady was the curveball that made her reconsider everything. "You have no idea how much that means."

"Are you on your way downstairs?" he asked, noticing her bags.

"I was heading out."

"May I help you with your bags?"

"That's so kind of you," she said. "But are you sure you're okay? I don't want to put you to work if you're supposed to be taking it easy."

"You sound like my wife. I promise to only help you get them to the lobby. Maureen can take over from there." He lifted the handle of the larger of her suitcases and picked up her small duffel bag.

Alexa picked up her purse and took the handle of her smaller roller bag. She gave the room one more once-over before shutting the door behind her. The two of them rode the elevator down and he helped her get the bags to the lobby, like he'd said. He got Maureen's attention and she came over with a cart to take the bags to the shuttle.

Quinn was at the front desk when Gavin walked her over to check out. He didn't smile as she approached.

"Ms. Fox is checking out," Gavin said to Quinn, who didn't say anything in return.

Alexa turned over the key to the room while Quinn typed some things into the computer, avoiding eye contact. She glanced to the right, where Nora was standing. She didn't make eye contact with Alexa, either.

It was probably for the best. She didn't want to make things any more awkward than they already were. Quinn printed out a receipt and handed it to her.

"That's it?" Gavin asked Quinn.

"Thanks for staying at the Seasons Inn," Quinn muttered.

Gavin gave Alexa one of those small smiles that Brady had given her a million times this week. "Have a safe trip home, Ms. Fox. And we hope you'll come back and visit us someday."

She so badly wanted to say she would love to come back, but there was no way she could do that if Brady didn't want to see her again, and seeing how Quinn and Nora felt about her, there was little chance that was happening. "Thank you," she replied, then headed outside to get on the shuttle into town.

BRADY HAD BEEN avoiding the inn all morning. He knew Alexa was checking out today and he was doing everything in his power to make sure he didn't see her before she left. He had spent the whole afternoon and evening yesterday looking over his shoulder, hoping she wouldn't show her face. He might have also been hoping she *would* show her face. He knew it was best if he didn't see her again, but that didn't stop him from wanting to see her.

He wouldn't have gone to the lobby if his mother hadn't asked him to go look for his father, who was supposed to be home resting. Brady found him standing at the front desk with Quinn.

"Mom is not happy with you for ignoring the doctor's orders to take a couple of days off."

"I'm not working," his dad said, standing there in his uniform.

"You look like you're working to me."

"I think he just wanted to make sure one guest in particular checked out," Quinn said. "He basically escorted her out."

Their dad scowled at Quinn. "I did not escort her out. I helped her with her bags."

Alexa was gone. For some reason that didn't give Brady the peace he had hoped it would. Instead, there was part of him that wanted to run out front to see if she was still there. He hated that things had ended the way they did. The need for a real goodbye wasn't lessened by his anger at her.

"Did you say anything to her?"

"Dad was way nicer than I would have been," Quinn said.

"I believe her," their dad said. "I don't think she plans to do anything with all that information you saw on her computer. I think she wants us to own the inn for as long as we want."

Brady was caught off guard. "What makes you say that?"

"I had a good talk with her about what happened yesterday, about the proposal, about *you*."

His heart wasn't going to handle this well, but he had to ask. "You talked to her about me?"

"I did. Good thing I did. She has some ideas

about how we can protect ourselves from investors who don't have our best interests at heart. She is going to send them to me so we can look them over."

"Is it smart to trust someone who works for a company that eats little businesses like ours for breakfast?" Nora asked, coming over to the front desk.

Their dad shrugged. "I don't know about that, but I think it's smart to trust someone who is falling in love with your son."

Brady froze. His dad's declaration had practically knocked the wind out of him. "What?"

His dad grabbed him by the shoulders. "That woman isn't going to come after our inn. She is head over heels for you. There isn't any way she would do anything that would put what you love in jeopardy."

A million thoughts ran through Brady's head. He had so many questions. The main one being why did his dad sound so sure about that? "I don't know how you could know that."

"I don't know how you couldn't," his dad countered. "It's right there written all over her face the moment she starts talking about you."

"I saw it, too," Nora chimed in. "It's really hard to believe that she could feel that way and still go back to New York and advise someone to come take all this away from us."

"She's been busted. Of course she's not going to do anything anymore. We're onto her and she knows we wouldn't do business with her investment firm if she begged," Quinn argued.

Their dad frowned. "It makes me sad that you're such a cynic."

Brady tried to digest everything that was being said. His dad and sister thought Alexa was telling the truth. Quinn thought they had simply foiled her plans. Clearly, his heart wanted it to be the way his dad and sister saw it, but he worried that Quinn could be right.

"She's taking the shuttle into town to pick up her rental car at the repair shop. She might still be waiting out there," Gavin said, nodding toward the door.

It was an internal battle for the ages. If he went out there and found her, it could be the best decision he ever made, or it could just make everything worse. His dad didn't know her. He couldn't know what she was capable of. She could simply be an amazing actress for all he knew. Nora was a hopeless romantic. It made sense that she would want to believe Alexa was truly in love with him. Quinn didn't let emotions get in the way. He was also a cynic, like their dad had said. His own negative experiences tainted how he viewed other people's relationships. Maybe Alexa cared about Brady enough not to do anything that would hurt his family.

There was only one way to find out. He left his family standing there to go find her, but she wasn't outside. Maureen informed him that the shuttle had just left. Brady couldn't let her leave town without knowing if his dad and sister were right. He ran back inside and asked Quinn for his car keys. He was the only one who kept them on him at all times.

Reluctantly, his older brother handed them over. Brady raced back to the parking lot and went in search of the truth.

Alexa needed to make one stop before she could bring herself to leave town. Maple Peak was on her way and she knew exactly how to get there. She would ride the lift up to the summit, take in the views one last time, and hike to the waterfall so she could scream her frustrations until her lungs gave out.

It wasn't as fun to ride up without Brady, but that was something she needed to get used to. She wasn't going to be doing anything with Brady in the future. Their time together was up.

The ski mountain was a bit more crowded today than the last time. Most people were headed to the first stop halfway up the mountain, where the zip line was located. Alexa had hoped that she and Brady might get to go ziplining someday. Alone, nothing sounded very fun.

At the summit, families and groups were taking pictures and oohing and aahing over the scenery below. Alexa went to the spot with the best view of Lake Champney. She knew she wouldn't be able to see the inn, but she knew it was there. Under the cover of the sugar maples and fir trees was the place that had stolen her heart.

Alexa couldn't linger. She needed to finish her goodbye tour and hit the road. It was a long drive back to Manhattan. She followed the trail that they had taken just a couple of days before that led to Bobcat Falls.

The sound of the water caught her attention first. She was close. Although there had been more people at the summit than Friday, there was no one on the hiking trail. This was good since she was about to make a fool of herself and yell at a waterfall.

When she arrived at the base of the falls, she took one more glance around before she balled up her fists and threw her head back. "I love Brady Seasons!" she shouted at the roaring water. The words had come out so easily it surprised her. How could she be in love with someone she just met? How else could she explain why she felt the way she did? Leaving Apple Hollow with him thinking the very worst of her was excruciating. He had been the first person in so long to see her the way she wanted to see herself.

All she could do now was try her best to be that person. The alternative of going back and falling into her old routine was enough to make her sick. She couldn't give up the idea that there was a balance out there. A way to live her life that brought her joy instead of this awful feeling of regret.

She let the waterfall mist hit her face for another minute. She couldn't leave Apple Hollow full of so much regret. She needed to see Brady one more time and try to explain herself. Maybe he would listen, maybe he wouldn't, but she couldn't run away and act like none of what had happened between them this week mattered. That was what the old Alexa would have done. She would have pushed aside her feelings and forced herself to get lost in her work. New and improved Alexa was going to fight to be happy.

The rocky path was blocked, however, by a familiar face.

"You've got to be kidding," Alexa said under her breath. There in the path was that moose. Now, she couldn't be a hundred percent sure it was the same moose from the other day or the same moose from the ATV trail or the same moose from the road, but it glowered at her just like they had.

These creatures were not supposed to come out during the day. What had she done to draw them out in the open? Was her perfume a secret moose attractant?

She stared it down, trying to remember how Brady handled it when they came face-to-face with this animal. He always talked to it. "Go back in the woods, where it's safe. Go on now. I have places to be. I can't stay on this mountain all day."

The moose gave her a little snort.

"Hey, I am not having the best day, okay? Can you please move along so I can find the guy that I've fallen in love with and let him know that he means everything to me?"

"You're in love with me?" a voice said from behind her.

Alexa whipped around, and there in all his sunshine glory was Brady. She rubbed her eyes to make sure she wasn't seeing things.

"What are you doing here?" she asked him when she was sure it was really him.

"You answer my question first."

It was one thing to want to tell him how she felt; it was much harder to do it. "I was trying to reason with the moose so I could get down the mountain."

Brady stepped closer. "I heard that."

"I thought maybe he'd understand that a desperate woman is no one to mess with."

Brady put his hands on his hips. "I'm not sure I would mess with you on a good day."

His playful banter was giving her the hope she needed to be honest. "I've been falling in love with you since that first day when you so graciously forgave me for hitting you with a grape, and when you came to find me when I got separated from the paddleboarding group and you told me we should be partners. I want people in my life that look out for me, forgive me when I'm sorry, and care about making the world a better place. No one does that better than you. So, yes, I told Mr. Moose over there that I'm in love with you because it's true."

Brady nodded. "Well, to answer your question, I've been following you since you left the inn, trying to catch up to you to find out if there was any possibility that I was wrong and you were being honest with me when you said you wanted to do the right thing for the inn. Quinn thinks there's no way it could be a big misunderstanding."

"Your brother isn't as smart as he thinks he is."

He laughed and shrugged, like perhaps she

was right about that. "My dad and sister believe you."

Alexa's chest lightened. "Those two, however, are very smart. Not to mention, your sister does have superpowers."

Brady took another step closer. "Do you want to know why they believe you?"

He was too close for her to think straight anymore. Alexa nodded her head, hoping they weren't the only two Seasonses to believe in her.

"They told me that you were in love with me," he said. Alexa wanted to scream it again so he would know it was true. "I wasn't so sure." He took the last step to put himself inches away from her. "But when I heard you tell the moose, I realized that maybe they were onto something."

"I told the waterfall, too, if you need a little more proof."

Brady placed his hand on her cheek. "Well, that does it. You must be falling for me."

Alexa swallowed hard. She wanted nothing more than this. For him to know she never meant him any harm. "I also wasn't going to let—"

Before she could finish, Brady was pressing his lips against hers. She threw her arms around his neck. Actually, she had wanted some of this, too. Kissing Brady was at the top of the list of things that made Alexa happy. Knowing he might feel the same sent her over the moon.

Brady pulled back. "Sorry, I've been wanting to do that since I heard you tell the moose how you felt about me. I couldn't wait one more second."

Her head was spinning in a haze of happiness. "I just wanted you to know that I will never let anything happen to the inn."

"I believe that, too." His grin told her he meant it; the kiss he gave her convinced her that he was sure. Brady stopped kissing her and pulled out his phone. He put his arm around Alexa and held the phone up to take a selfie. "Smile, Mr. Moose," he said before taking the picture. Then he turned to the moose. "Okay, buddy, I love her, too. You can move along now."

The moose grunted and lifted his head and lowered it as if he was saying he understood before slowly walking back into the woods.

CHAPTER TWENTY

BRADY LED THE group of paddleboarders back to the shore. "And that is the tour of Lake Champney. We're going to bring everything up to the beach and I'll take all your equipment."

He checked his watch. This was his last activity of the day, and he couldn't wait for what the rest of the day had in store.

Kayden came jogging down. "I'll take care of the equipment for you."

He was the best; Brady was so grateful. "Thanks, man."

They were putting up the decorations for the Labor Day party later this weekend. Ivy was busy setting up red, white, and blue balloon arches around the patio. While he had been on the lake, someone had hung pleated patriotic flag fans from the windows that faced the lake. String lights had been strung back and forth across the lawn.

He took off for the main building to let Ivy know that one of the flag fans had come unattached on one side. She wasn't anywhere to be seen, so he went inside to look for her. He went in through the dining room and made his way toward the lobby to see if she was in her office that was near there.

As soon as he made it around the corner, there she was chatting with Quinn and Nora. Not Ivy. *Alexa*. Her hair was down and she had on a long red dress that she would need to change out of if she was going to come with him on the adventure he had planned. Still, she made his heart pitter-patter in a way no one else could.

He came up behind her and picked her up off her feet. "You're early."

Her laugh made him even happier that she was finally here. He set her down so she could turn around and give him a hug.

"I wish I would have left even earlier. The traffic getting out of the city was a nightmare, especially with a car full of so much stuff. I couldn't even see out of the back window."

Brady held her tighter, even though he didn't have to worry about not being able to do this whenever he wanted to anymore. Alexa was here and she was here to stay. After going back to New York in June, she left Gatton Investments and joined a prestigious consulting firm that businesses hired to save them from going under.

She had only been working there a month and

she absolutely loved it. The best part of that job was she could work remotely from anywhere in the world. Thankfully, Alexa decided that the place that made her happiest was Apple Hollow and she bought a little lakeside cottage on the west side of Lake Champney. It had green siding a couple shades darker than her eyes and a back deck that offered her the most gorgeous view of the lake.

"I'm so glad you're here," he said, happy they would never have to love each other from long distance again.

"I missed you," she said as she hummed in contentment. He stood back so that he could see the face he'd been dreaming about since he'd visited Alexa in New York at the beginning of August.

The smile she unleashed on him forced him to have to kiss his way up her neck so she could wear it a little longer.

"Brady, not in the lobby." She giggled and gave him a little push.

"Yeah, could you please take this reunion somewhere private if it's going to turn into a full-on make-out session?" Quinn said from behind the counter.

Brady's siblings were both truly happy for him. Their dad had shared the information Alexa had emailed him about how to protect the inn.

They followed her steps and were feeling pretty confident that they would be able to keep the inn in the family for a long time to come. That was all it took to win over Quinn. Nora had been sold long ago.

"I knew you weren't planning to come by the house until later, so I stopped here to steal you away sooner. Is that okay?"

"Anytime you want to steal me away, it's okay."

That breathtaking smile was back and she took him by the hand. They said their goodbyes to Quinn and Nora, with promises of being back for family dinner tonight.

Alexa's new car was filled with all the stuff she hadn't trusted the movers to get there safely. The movers were due at the house in a few hours, which was when he had expected to see Alexa. They drove over to the house, which was minutes from the inn.

Brady grabbed some things from the trunk while Alexa went to unlock the door to her new home. She pushed open the door and he heard her squeal with joy.

He loved how excited she was about owning her first house. She ran back out and grabbed her own load of items to carry in. They unpacked and talked about how the plans were going for the very first Seasons at the Lake, which was going to take place this winter. They decided they needed more time to do things right, so they made the winter season the first of the four. Alexa was full of ideas for how to promote all the winter activities. The fact that she would be here to help and see it come together meant everything to him.

Once they unloaded the car, Brady went to the refrigerator that he had already stocked with drinks, knowing they had a busy day of unpacking ahead of them.

"You thought of everything," she said, opening the bottle of her favorite soda. She took a long drink and let out a satisfied "Ahhh."

"I have a housewarming gift for you. Do you want to open it now or after the movers get here?"

She scrunched up her brow. "Are you really asking that question? Of course I want to open it now!"

Brady had brought over his surprise a couple of days ago in preparation of her arrival. He went into the bedroom where he had hidden it. The present was wrapped in paper the color of Alexa's eyes—greens and blues swirled together.

"I thought that you needed to have something in your house to remind you of the day you decided to make choices based on what brought you joy."

Alexa quietly clapped her hands together. Her face was equal parts curiosity and excitement. He set it down in front of her and she unwrapped it like he used to rip open his Christmas presents when he was a kid. Her eagerness made him laugh.

As soon as she saw what it was, her eyes welled with tears. "Oh, Brady," she said, holding the framed photo of the two of them by the waterfall with the moose in the background.

"I also wanted to make sure that anyone who comes to visit you has proof that you have seen a moose."

She set it down and practically tackled him. "I love you so much," she said, burying her face in his neck.

"Not as much as I love you," he replied, inhaling the scent of her hair. He was never going to have to miss this again.

She let go of him and narrowed her eyes. "Did you just attempt to out-love me?"

He shrugged. "I mean, I can't lie. What do you want me to say?"

"I wouldn't challenge me to a love-off, Brady Seasons. You'll lose."

He cocked his head to the side. "Would it really be losing to be loved the most?"

She had to think about that for a minute. "Be loved more or be the bigger lover...hmm."

"Sounds like no matter what, we both win."

She gave him a kiss. "That's the way it should always be."

There were no doubts it would.

* * * * *

Harlequin® Reader Service

Enjoyed your book?

Try the perfect subscription for Romance readers and get more great books like this delivered right to your door.

See why over 10+ million readers have tried Harlequin Reader Service.

Start with a Free Welcome Collection with free books and a gift—valued over $20.

Choose any series in print or ebook.
See website for details and order today:

TryReaderService.com/subscriptions